A compelling story chronicling the perils of a young girl as she embarks on a new life when leaving her small town for 'city life' and a career after she completes her college education.

Written by Cora A. Seaman

Cover/Layout by Barbara E. Zwickel - Aztec Printing, Inc.

PUBLISHED BY

731 C. Erie Ave. • Evansville, Indiana 47715

www.cordonpublications.com

cora.seaman@hotmail.com

(812) 303-9070

Published by Cora A. Seaman in conjunction with Cordon Publications

First printing: December, 2011

Printed in the United States of America

ISBN: 978-1-937912-00-0

ebook: 978-1-937912-01-7 e-book

To: Morgin

Lilli

by Cora A. Seaman

Cora J. Seaman

9/14

Cora A. Seaman

DEDICATION

This story is dedicated to my husband,
Don who faithfully edits and corrects my
faulty grammar, and continues to
encourage me to keep on writing.

Cora A. Seaman

LILLI ELAYNE
Chapter 1

Lilli knew how old she was, and she knew when her birthday was, but what she didn't know was just who her real mother and father were. She had heard rumors of many things that had happened when she was born, but she couldn't be sure of any of them. How could she tell which of the stories were true? And which of those stories were just someone's active imagination? She would have to discover the truth for herself.

Lilli was born on January 1, 1900. She could always remember that she was born on New Years Day when an old century had ended and it was the first day of a new century. Mother always told her that it was an omen to have such a memorable birthday. But what was an omen? Lilli never understood what an omen meant. If being born on New Years Day was a good omen, then she would hopefully benefit from it. However, if it were a bad omen, then, what could that mean to Lilli?

Regardless of omens, good or bad, Lilli was destined to survive in a world that seemed to toss her about in her effort to become a woman, a wife, a mother, and above all else, the answer to the question that had haunted her all of her life.

Chapter 2

It had been a cruel winter in the latter part of 1899 for the family of George and Lula Jackson. Their small cabin nestled in the woods near Otwell, Indiana, seemed to leak cold air from every crevice. The windows were boarded over to keep out the wicked wind during the season when it seemed to blow from night until morning. The door that was ill fitting in good weather seemed to invite more cold air to seep into their home no matter how many old rugs they pushed against it. A raging fire in the fireplace didn't seem to be able to counteract the ravages of the fierce weather raging outside their humble home.

George had cut and stored wood for their winter needs throughout the summer and fall, stacking it near the entrance to the cabin. The winter had been a long one and most of their firewood had been used. He worried that they might have to start burning the furniture if the weather didn't let up soon.

Lula was expecting their first child. She was not doing well during her pregnancy. She had gained an enormous amount of weight, a lot more than her small frame could handle. She was only sixteen years old. She and George had been married on her sixteenth birthday in February, 1899, and it seemed as if she became pregnant immediately. George did not have brothers or sisters so he did not know what to expect from a pregnant woman. He was worried about Lula and how she had been feeling, but he was unequipped to be of much help. He was convinced that he should have taken her to a doctor, but there was no money for such expenses. George knew that she was young and strong. He never feared for a moment that she would weather this type of storm as well.

The Jackson's had a small piece of farm land out in the country near Otwell. George had inherited the farm from his father, and after his father's death, George had managed to clear about five additional acres of the land. He planted it in a garden for their use. He raised enough crops to feed a milk cow, a few pigs, and his two horses. The year of 1899 had been a year of severe drought so the crops did not fare very well. However, he was able to help Lula preserve enough vegetables that they thought that they would have enough food to eat through the winter, but the food for the animals was almost gone. He wondered just what he would do if they ran out of hay for the animals. But, he couldn't think of that now; he needed to tend to Lula.

Otwell, Indiana, was not a big city. In fact, it was only a small community. It was located off the main road and was home to no more than ten families. The land around the community was 'scrub land' which meant that it wasn't good for much. A good farmer could make enough on his farm to feed his family but rarely made enough to sell to the merchants in the nearest town of Jasper. The community was surrounded by forests that provided homes to many kinds of wildlife including bear, deer, wild turkeys, rabbits, foxes, and bobcats. The streams nearby, which were offshoots of the White River, were filled with fish. Many of the streams had badger and beaver that lived in them. The farmers often caught the wild animals and sold their pelts in Jasper for enough money to buy staples for the home. George was a good hunter. There was no shortage of meat for their table during the winter. And he could usually sell enough pelts to provide his family with the extras that they needed during the winter. He knew how to get a mess of fish for their dinner or hunt a rabbit for a sumptuous stew. But he worried about the farm animals. If he couldn't feed the cow, then there would be no milk. He knew that they needed milk for the baby who would soon be born.

Chapter 3

George Jackson had grown up in the Otwell area. His father had been a school teacher at the one room school just down the road from where George and Lula had built their cabin. George had attended the school with his father as his teacher until he was in the eighth grade. On November 4, 1894, his father was attacked by a bobcat as he was returning from a fishing trip on the White River. When he didn't return home for supper, George went looking for him. He found his body along a path in the woods. It was clear that he had been attacked by an angry animal and left for dead. George was confident that it was a bobcat because of the claw and bite marks on his father's face. The bobcat apparently wanted the fish that his father had been carrying because the fishing pole and line were dragged into the edge of a thicket. As George was trying to figure out how to get his father's body home, he spied two fierce eyes staring at him from the low hanging branch of a tree. He stopped for an instant and pondered what his next move should be. He knew that his father always carried a pistol but he was afraid if he reached for his father's body again the 'cat' might pounce on him. He watched the 'cat' for a few more minutes and neither of them moved a muscle. George knew that he was no match for the cat, and yet he knew that if he tried to turn and run, the cat would surely attack him. He had to do something. But what? He could not remove his father's body with the cat watching him. He couldn't leave the body out in the wild for the night or for other animals to drag it away. He held the lantern high to get a better look at his father's body to see if he could see the pistol. Suddenly, he saw that his father had probably tried to shoot the animal since the pistol was in his right hand.

George fell to his knees, still clutching the lantern, and slowly crept to the side of his father. He could feel the eyes of the 'cat' boring into his flesh and he hoped that all that he had to endure was the evil gaze of the cat not its unforgiving thirst for blood.

He reached for the pistol and leveled it at the cat. He pulled the trigger and blasted the cat out of the tree. He was not dead, but he was wounded enough that he was not able to attack him. George walked to the wounded animal and finished the job that apparently his father had tried to do before he was fatally attacked. George pulled the cat back into the woods a few feet, then went to his father's mortally wounded body and lifted it to his horse. He had the unpleasant chore of telling his mother that she was now a widow.

When George told his mother that her husband had been mauled by a bobcat, she was inconsolable. She continued to cry and mourn him for several days. When they held a service for him at the local church, she could not force herself to attend. She had remained at home in seclusion, unable to face the reality. George had no siblings. He was now the sole support of his mother. He worked their farm as best that he could. He hunted and fished for food for their table. He harvested the crops that he had planted and took care of the animals in the barn. In fact, he became 'his father' to his mother. She seemed unable to function since her husband's death. Early one morning in September, George found his mother in the barn, hanging from a rope that they used to hoist the hay up to the loft. She was no longer grieving for her husband; she had joined him in death.

In less than one year, George lost both his mother and father, making him an orphan. He was only fourteen years old.

Chapter 4

When he and Lula married, he brought her home to his cabin to live. It was the best he could offer her.

Lula had no training on how to be a mother. When she and George were married, she told him that she didn't know much about being a wife and mother. Her mother and father were quite elderly. Although she was only sixteen when they married, her parents were in their 50's when she was born. Before Lula could have her baby, a neighbor came to tell her that her parents had been taken to the "Pike County Poor Farm" to live. They were no longer able to care for themselves.

The Pike County Poor Farm was an establishment that was operated by the Township Trustee's office of the county government. When a family could no longer support themselves, they could relinquish all their belongings to the county. In exchange for all their earthly possessions, the county would give them a place to live for the remainder of the lives. The Poor Farms were a fixture in Indiana at the turn of the century. It was not uncommon for a family to spend the end of their days on a farm working for their room and board after having sacrificed their entire livelihood that they had amassed since their youth. While it seemed like a cruel way to spend their lives, it was the only recourse that many farm families had for their retirement. Although the concept seemed cruel and unusual punishment, many families thrived in the environment that gave them the opportunity to continue to work on a farm, or do repair work around the 'home'. The women continued to cook, clean, and harvest and preserve the vegetables and fruits grown on the property. It seemed that this was the same thing that most of them had been doing during their younger years except for the fact that they now had no worries about how they would heat their cabin in the winter or provide for the livestock if the crops failed. Lula's parents were content to have a place to live with no demands on their lives. Her mother's mind had been wandering for several years. She seemed to be unaware of the impending birth of her grandchild. She often wandered away from home and Lula's father had to search for her, sometimes into the night. He had spent many years working on the farm, but had become so feeble that he could not continue to care for his aging wife at home. The opportunity to relinquish the farm in exchange for a place for the two of them to live and to receive care for his wife. It all seemed to be a blessing to Lula's father.

Chapter 5

Lula had been sick almost every day since she had discovered that she was pregnant. She had not seen a doctor so she had no idea that this was not normal to be sick all the time. She seemed to be swollen many times her usual size. Her legs seemed to be so swollen that she could hardly walk. It was impossible for her to get shoes on her feet, so she wore the shoes that George had nearly worn threadbare. Her hands and face were swollen too. Some days she could hardly get her eyes open to see.

Lula wanted to be a good wife for George. She tried to cook meals for him, but was unable to stand on her feet for more than a few minutes. She wanted to make biscuits for him each morning, but would only get them in the oven, and then she would be forced to go to bed. He seemed to understand how she must feel. But, he wondered what he would do when it came time to deliver their baby. He knew where the mid-wife lived a few miles down the road. He would get her if he saw there was going to be trouble with the birth. He had helped to birth many animals on the farm, but assisting in the birth of his own baby might be more than he could handle. He barely knew the neighbors just to the east of their farm. Their names were Andy and Mary Jane Horton. He had met them when it was time to thresh the wheat a few years ago. He had helped them on their farm, and they came to help him get his hay in before the rains came. He had heard his father talk about what good neighbors they had been to him. He was sure he could depend on them to help him with the birthing if he needed them. The Horton's attended the same country church where George and Lula had been going. However, George and Lula had not been able to attend church since Lula had been so sick.

George was fairly sure he could birth a baby just like you birth a baby calf. He had done that many times. The provisions for their baby were sparse. Lula had not been able to sew many things for the impending birth. She only had prepared a few 'feed sacks' that could be used for diapers. As the time for her delivery drew nearer, she worried that she would not be able to care for the baby at all. She tried to convince herself that the excess weight would go away immediately after the birth. She never mentioned her worries to George, since he was quite concerned about how they would survive the winter.

Shortly before Christmas, Lula began to bleed short spots of blood on her underwear. She was not sure what this might mean, but she waited to see if it stopped or if it was going to get worse. She wondered if she should send George to get the doctor, but how could they pay him. They had very little for themselves, and nothing to give to anyone else. Lula silently cried in desperation at their plight. She didn't know what she could do to ease the situation. She was eating as little food as she could, but knew that she had to eat enough to sustain the child inside of her.

Chapter 6

Early one morning, Lula awakened George to tell him that she was in extreme pain. He soon discovered that there was water everywhere in the bed. He knew what that meant. Her water sack had broken and the birth of the baby was imminent. He hurried to the kitchen and stoked the fire to make the house warm for the birth of the baby. He knew that he would need hot water. He searched for the towels, blankets, and rags that he knew that Lula had managed to have ready for when the baby came. He knew there were not many baby clothes, but he was sure that blankets would work for clothes until they could sell a calf or a pig for extra money. He hurried back to help Lula, who by this time, was in almost unbearable pain. He could see that she was having a really hard time. He saw her breathing was slowing and that her hands were trembling. She continued to scream, but her screams were growing fainter each time that she cried out. Finally, he could see the baby was coming. He helped deliver the baby and cut the cord. He wrapped the infant in a blanket and began to tend to Lula. She was bleeding profusely. It seemed that all her blood had drained from her body. Her skin was cool to the touch and it appeared to be turning white. He knew she was in trouble. He leaned over to tell her that he would go get the mid-wife, but she wrapped her arms around him and whispered for him to take care of the baby. She turned to the window as the tears ran down her cheeks. Then she breathed her last breath.

George was devastated. How could this happen? He wanted to be a good husband. What was he to do with a baby that he had no idea how to care for, including feeding her. He realized that he had wrapped the child in a blanket without washing the birthing liquid from it. And, he didn't even know if his baby was a boy or girl. He lifted the bundle from the bedside and took it to the kitchen where the fire was warming the room. He opened the bundle and saw a beautiful baby girl, looking back at him. She began to cry, no doubt asking for something to eat. George quickly sponged off the baby's body and wrapped it in another blanket. He leaned over and kissed the child. It was his own flesh and blood. But how could he raise a child alone? He sat down at the kitchen table with a cup of cold coffee and tried to think. He was oblivious to the fact that the baby was still crying. He needed a plan. What could he do? Maybe he should share his dilemma with the Hortons.

He bundled the baby in the blanket, pulled on his own coat and boots and started out the door. It was about a half mile down to the Horton's house. He had already decided that he would go there. He straddled his horse, bareback, and clutching the baby, rode off toward the neighbor's house. He knocked on the door and when Mary Jane answered, he thrust his bundle into her hands and told her that Lula had died while giving birth to this baby. He knew that she could help him until he could make other plans. He was visibly shaken. Mary Jane took the still crying baby and invited him inside. He refused her offer and as he returned to his horse he whipped it into a running frenzy trying to get back to his now deceased wife.

George went into their bedroom. It reeked of blood, birthing fluid, and death. Lula was still lying on the bed with the look of death on her face. She was cold and colorless. He reached over and pulled her eyelids down to close her eyes. He pulled the covers over her face to hide it from himself. He could hardly bear to touch her. He had buried his father and his mother, but this was his wife. Did he have to bury her too? He stood at the edge of the bed, holding the cold, clammy hand of his precious wife, and cried until he could cry no more tears. What would he do without her and how could he raise their baby daughter? He closed his eyes and could see the smiling face of the tiny infant that he had just helped to birth. How could he tend to the farm and raise a baby, too. He didn't know anything about how to take care of an infant. How could he feed her? Did Lula have baby bottles somewhere? Of course not, she would have breast fed the baby. How do you feed a baby when the mother can't, he asked himself? And, who would he call on to get the answer to his questions? He was almost beside himself with unanswered questions. What should he do first?

George knew the next thing that he had to do was to

go to the undertaker and arrange for a burial for Lula. He would bury her next to his mother in the church cemetery. This time, with less panic, he saddled his horse and rode into town to find the undertaker.

Chapter 7

The wagon with its precious cargo, pulled by one of the horses from the farm, wound its way down the narrow, rutted road to the cemetery. George was driving the horse as he tried to make the trip as pleasant as possible for its rider, even though she would never know how hard he had tried. The snow had stopped as if it knew that it was time to let up for a few hours so that this woman who had given her life while giving life to another, could be buried on a nicer day than she had seen for weeks. There were several neighbors gathered around the open grave awaiting the widower to bring the body for burial. Someone, unknown to George, sang a hymn and a minister said a few words about heaven and God as the group huddled together to try to ward off the cold wind. It was a solemn ceremony and a quiet crowd. There were no answers for the questions that everyone wanted answered, and no one was asking them.

George waited for the service to be completed then he walked to the head of the grave and placed a crudely fashioned cross there with the name: **Lula Elayne Jackson, 1884-1900** into the ground. He turned and walked to his wagon and headed for home.

He entered the empty house that seemed to echo as he walked across the floor. He went back to the kitchen and poured another cup of cold coffee. He looked around the room to see what he thought of this place, without his wife. Their life together had been so short. He married her when she was just a child. She was a beautiful girl whom he loved dearly. She wanted to be his wife, but she was sick. She didn't know why she could not seem to shake the illness that apparently was the cause of her death. Now, his life seemed empty. Yet, he was a father. That thought left him baffled. He wasn't prepared to be a father without a wife.

He went to their room and gathered up the soiled bedding. He carried the mess to the kitchen. He slowly put it in the cook stove and burned it. He walked around the house and chose the things that he thought were important to him. He took the Bible that his mother had given him as a child and he wrote in the front: Lula Elayne Jackson, deceased January 1, 1900. Daughter, Lilli Elayne Jackson, born January 1, 1900. He closed the Bible and stuffed it inside his coat. He picked up the knapsack of belongings that he had collected and walked out the door. He closed the door and locked it with a large brass key, given him by his father. He saddled up his horse and rode over to the Horton's house. He knocked on the door and when Mary Jane answered, he stepped inside. He handed her a slip of paper on which he had written, Lilli Elayne, January 1, 1900. He handed her the brass key.

"What is this for, George?" Mary Jane asked.

"It isn't much, Mrs. Horton, but it is all that I have. I am giving you my baby, and my home. Please raise her as your own." With that admonishment, he turned and walked out the door. He mounted his strawberry roan horse and headed west, urging the horse into a gallop as the two of them went down the same rutted road that they had traveled less than 3 hours ago. They passed the church cemetery where George had buried his young wife, but he turned away.

He did not want to see the grave or the marker listing her name. He continued on toward the western sunset and to parts unknown to him. That was the last time anyone in Otwell could ever remember seeing George Jackson again.

Chapter 8

Mary Jane and Andrew Horton were astonished at what had just happened. They had no provisions for a baby, but Andy quickly brought in from the barn, a crude wooden box. Mary Jane lined it with a heavy quilt and placed the newborn baby girl inside. Andy took the brass key over to the house and looked for baby clothes. He had hoped to find a few. He wasn't disappointed, a few was all that he found. He returned with a nightgown for the baby, and a few feed sacks that he was sure Lula had meant to use as diapers. They had been scrubbed on the washboard until they were soft and cut to size for a newborn. They were hemmed rather crudely by a helpless young mother who was doing all that she could to prepare for her baby. However, one thing that they needed immediately was baby bottles. Mary Jane had warmed a little milk on the stove and dipped her finger in the liquid, allowing Lilli to suck it from the tip of her finger. She didn't know how else she could feed the crying little waif. After a few minutes, the baby had stopped crying. She was such a beautiful baby. Her hair was light and silky like corn silks. She appeared to have blue eyes, although, she had cried so hard, her eyes were barely open. Her round, pink face featured high cheekbones and light eyebrows. Her hands were clinched in a tight fist but her long fingers were not hidden from view. Mary Jane had never had a baby, so she reveled in this experience.

How could she have been so lucky to be given a baby? Then she realized that a woman had given her life for this child. She bowed her head and prayed for the soul of the mother and gave thanks for the blessing of a child. Indeed the Horton's would raise the child as their own. Lilli Elayne Horton had a good sound to it. No one would ever need to know about the method that the Horton's had become her parents. It was still a closed community at least for the year 1900.

LILLI ELAYNE
Chapter 9

I have already told you that I was a waif, given to the neighbors when I was less than a week old.

As Lilli, I began to grow like weeds in a vegetable garden. I was quite a gregarious child. My inquisitive nature made me want to experience everything around me as I began to mature.

I attended the one room school that was just down the road from where I lived. I walked to school if the winter weather wasn't too ferocious. If the snow was deep enough to be over my boot tops, Dad loaded me in the wagon and took me to school. At the school, the teacher constantly corrected my behavior. He reported to my parents that I would not sit quietly in the classroom and that I disrupted the other children's ability to learn. I firmly denied these accusations, but the teachers always won the debate.

When my tenth birthday arrived, Dad gave me a pony. I had to stand on a box to mount him, but I fell in love with my pony whom I named Jimmy. He became my best friend. Working in the garden or in the barn with Dad was fun for me. I loved watching the flowers and vegetables grow, but it was more fun to ride down the road on Jimmy.

I was beginning to grow both in stature and emotionally. It became obvious to Mother that I needed to change the way my clothing was made for me. I resented being forced to wear aprons over straight dresses and continued to request more stylish dresses like some of the other children were wearing. When Mother would take me to Jasper on her shopping trips, I rushed to the library to see the magazines that featured the latest fashions. I wanted to look like those women, not like a little country girl. I continually asked to have a different hair style. Since I was quite small, my hair was braided into two long braids that hung down my back. I wanted curls and 'finger waves' like I had seen on the models in the magazines. When Mother refused to allow me these 'grown-up' styles, I took matters in my own hands.

One day, while she was in town getting supplies, she had left me alone in the house while she was gone. I quietly slipped into her bedroom and retrieved her scissors from her sewing basket. Standing on a stool before the mirror, I clipped the braids off at the nape of my neck. When the hair flared out from the braids, it was quite wavy. I loved the look but I still wanted it shorter. I continued to cut on my hair until I had a very short 'bob'. Then, I tried to make the waves in my hair like the models had in their hair; I couldn't seem to make it work right. I wondered just what would make it take the shape of a 'finger wave'. My only conclusion was the lard that Mother used for cooking which could help to hold the hair in place. A generous amount of lard smeared in my hair seemed to do the trick. In a short while, I had my hair styled just the way that I thought the other ladies had done their hair.

When Mother returned from town, she came into the house and was greeted by her daughter who had quite a stylish hair do, but was reeking of the lard smell. It would be fair to say at this point, that although Mother was a very patient person, this bit of insubordination did not sit well with her. Her first reaction was complete shock. After a few questions about how I had managed to cut my hair, she was furious that my hair was not only shortened beyond imagination, but was also smeared with an excess of her cooking condiment.

If she could have thought of a more devious method of punishment for me, I am not sure what it could have been. Instead of a 'switching' with a peach tree switch, which was my usual punishment, she took me to the barn, with a large pan of hot water and a generous amount of lye soap. She scrubbed my head repeatedly until she managed to get most of the lard out of my hair. Then, she changed the water and repeated the process. It took three heavy 'soapings' of that nasty smelling lye soap to get the heavy concentration of grease from my hair. When she had sufficiently removed the lard to her satisfaction, the hair style that remained was almost hilarious. She then returned to the house, plopped me down in the kitchen chair and began to try to style what was left of my shortened hair. It was a long time before the results of my attempt at hair styling grew out enough to be manageable. By that time, there were products on the market that could be used to style a woman's hair without using kitchen cooking products.

Chapter 10

By the time that I had finished my elementary education I was thirteen years old. I would be entering high school in 'downtown' Otwell the following fall. However, I was still a rebel when it came to my wardrobe. Mother had always wanted me to remain a small child, perhaps because I was the only child that she had, and she couldn't bear to watch me grow up. However, I was not content to be controlled by anyone and our confrontations only continued to grow into full blown conflicts. It was almost a case of: if she liked it, I didn't and if I liked it, she didn't. Most of our evenings after school were spent in disagreements over whatever the topic of conversation might be. It didn't matter.

Sports were not a big part of high school for me. Only the boys could play sports at that time. The girls were forced to take 'gym' while attending high school, but there was no organized sports program for the girls. The only outside activity that was part of the school curriculum available to us, was music. I had never had the opportunity to be exposed to music, but now I had a fierce desire to learn to play music. Whether I wanted to play music for the intrinsic value or whether I wanted to be included in some activity away from home, will always remain a mystery. Regardless of the reason, I begged my parents for a piano. It seemed like an innocent request to me; however, the family did not have adequate means to buy a piano. I settled for an old mandolin that my grandfather had played when he was young. I struggled to learn to play the thing, but any melody that it could produce eluded me. Finally Dad had a man come to our house and show me the basics of how to make music from this bulbous looking instrument. After a few short lessons, I was able to master playing that old 'beetle back mandolin'. I would sit on the porch, playing the mandolin, and singing "The Old Gray Mare" or "My Darling Clementine". Mother and Dad smiled their best smile of appreciation, but inside, I am sure that they were hoping that I soon would find another passion to pursue.

As usual, when we took a trip to Jasper, I left Mother at the store and headed for the Library. While I was browsing through the newspapers one morning, I saw the headlines that said: "Archduke Ferdinand, of the Austria-Hungarian Empire, Assassinated;" War declared on Germany. I was mesmerized at this bit of news. I really didn't have much knowledge of where this might be, but I was sure that anyone who was assassinated and was a leader of a foreign country, must be news. I continued to read the article and discovered how cruel the leaders of Germany really were. I wasn't very informed about the European countries, but I was anxious to learn more. I asked the woman at the library to show me a map. The two of us went to the wall where the librarian pulled down a large map on a roller, much like the window shades at our house. She pointed out to me just where the two countries were located. She continued to tell me about some of the happenings that were taking place. Many of the young people from Jasper and surrounding communities had already gone to Canada to join the Canadian Military Service so that they could help England and France fight for their rights. She explained that America was not in the war, that President Woodrow Wilson had campaigned for office with the promise that he would keep us out of war. The United States had not been included in any war effort. Any young man who wanted to fight in the war had to go to Canada or England and join their armed forces.

When we returned home, I was full of questions and information for Dad and Mother. She was not well informed about the war, but Dad seemed to know what was going on in Europe. He explained that the German leadership simply wanted to conquer the countries and control that portion of Europe. The Germans did agree with the leadership in the Austria-Hungarian Empire. But, they didn't expect other countries to join in the resistance.

The year was 1914; I was 14 years old.

Chapter 11

Even in 1918, graduation from high school at Otwell was quite a celebration. Most of the townspeople turned out for the event each spring. Because most of the men and many of the women had to work in the fields to get the crops planted, school was dismissed in mid-April. The weather usually was just beginning to show a little warmth. Summer was a long one, from May to September, and with no school work. However, the chores at home would occupy most of my time, day in and day out. I really never liked working in the garden or helping to preserve vegetables. But, it was a necessary chore to prepare enough food for winter when there was no other way to have food for the family. I began to wonder what life would hold for me. Soon I would find the answer to that question.

Chapter 12

The war in Europe had continued to be fought in a far off country, hardly identifiable by most of the people in Otwell, Indiana. I just didn't relate to what it was like to fight a war so far from home. President Wilson had assured us in 1912 that America would not enter the war. However, his promise to the American people would not be one that he could keep. In early 1917, the Germans sank our ship, The Lusitania, as it was sailing in the North Sea. Americans would not stand for this type of invasion. We soon rose to the challenge of doing our part in fighting off this enemy. Young men from all across the country flocked to the recruiting depots and signed on to go to this foreign country to fight. Otherwise, there was an active draft service commonly called the Selective Service.

Many of the young men left their farms and homes to join in the war effort. A lot of older men were also part of the enlistment quotas that were needed to fight this aggressive enemy who seemed so far away. Very few people knew where the battlefields were and the foreign sounding names did not clarify their locations. When soldiers had fought in the Civil War, the battlefields were evident by which state they were in. This was not the situation in WWI as this war came to be known. The soldiers, called doughboys, marched off to a foreign country in places they had never even heard of, but they were answering the call of their country. (The term "doughboys" came from the practice of carrying a ball of dough under their shirt so that it would 'rise' by the heat from their bodies. The process allowed them to have dough ready to make bread for their next meal.) The pictures that the soldiers sent back home were strange for the parents of my friends to understand. The pictures showed young men with hats that looked like a bowl on top of a piece of cardboard, and britches that flared above the knee, but stuffed into their boots. Many little boys had worn pants similar to these but they were called knickers. No one expected this style to be used for grown men as a military uniform.

The news of the war was fascinating to me. I begged Mother to let me go to the library and read the newspapers. She was not interested in the war news. Although she had no son in the war, many of her friends had someone in their family who was in some foreign country fighting.

Many of the young boys that had been in my class at school were now in the war; leaving Otwell almost barren of young men. I attended our church in the outskirts of town but most of the young people in the church were girls. Any of the boys who had not gone to war were young men who had to remain at home to help support their families on their farms.

Fortunately, for the town of Otwell, and many other small towns, our involvement in the war was not a long one. On November 11, 1918, the Allies, including the United States signed an Armistice with Germany and the "War to end all Wars ended." All the young men who had marched off to defend their country, now came marching home. Only a few from Pike County had been killed and their parents set about trying to cope with their losses. Many of the returning soldiers had stories to tell, and many others came home without arms or legs. And, the entire community mourned the ones who did not return but were buried in far away lands. Otwell lost one of its favorite sons when a fine young man named Norman Brandle was reported to have been killed in battle. He had been a big basketball hero for Otwell High School. His family lived on the road between our house and a town named Algiers. He had been only eighteen years old.

Chapter 13

I was glad to see the war end. It seemed to me that there was a pall over the community when all the young men were gone. During their absence, all of the mothers had one thing on their mind, praying for the day their sons would come home. Now perhaps things could return to normal. But, in my mind, I wondered what 'normal' really was for Otwell.

I was about to turn nineteen years old. I was beginning to think that I might like to find a real boyfriend. Many of the other girls in town had found a husband prior to the war; but I had not had much opportunity to find an eligible male within my group of friends.

I desperately wanted to go on to college. I approached Mother about my ability to go to Evansville and attend a college. I was discouraged from going on to school and urged to find a husband who would support me. I could settle down and raise a family right here in my own home town. But that isn't what I wanted to do. I did not want to be tied down with a family at the age of 19. I wanted to experience things and see places that I had read about in the Jasper library. As usual, I found it just as difficult to discuss this subject with her, as I had most other subjects. I had already perused the crowd of eligible bachelors and found none who would meet my criterion for a suitable suitor. I was determined not to become a farmer's wife. Their work was much too hard. Most of the men that I had met looked upon a woman as a hired helper. I had other plans for my future. I had hopes of becoming a school teacher. There did not seem to be an overabundance of them in our community. And, there was a rumor floating around Otwell that there was going to be a new school built on the outskirts of town. It was to be for the elementary school children. There were plans being discussed for bringing all the children from the surrounding communities into Otwell to attend this school. If this were to become a reality, they would need a lot of teachers. Maybe I could be one of them, I thought.

Chapter 14

Some of my friends from the church group were making plans to attend a college in Evansville. I had heard their plans discussed on several occasions. One of the girls from my graduating class, Vickie, was quite vocal about her plans. Her father had agreed to allow her to live in a dormitory on the campus of the school while she attended classes there. Those plans seemed so exciting to me. I would be away from the watchful eye of Mother and Father, and I would be free to do as I pleased. Vickie and I had been in the same class at high school. She continued to talk about going to college at all the parties and events that she would be participating in while she was a student at the college. She made the experience sound like a wonderful time to be having while also getting an education. I wanted to join her, but had no resources. I had already been told that there was no money available for me to go to college. What was I to do? I began to question Vickie about how she was going to pay for her education at the school. She explained to me that there were programs available for 'poor' people to go to college. I hated her phraseology when she categorized me as a 'poor' person, however truthful it was. But, if this was the truth, I would certainly qualify. She also mentioned that there were 'scholarships' available for people who could pass the test for a scholarship. I hurried home to try to find out more about this kind of program from the material that I had picked up at the library. If I could pass their test, then, perhaps I could go to college with Vickie.

I studied the information in the pamphlets that I had picked up at the library. They all explained how you could take a test and, perhaps, be considered for a scholarship to go to college. If you passed the test, the scholarship meant that all your expenses would be paid. I quickly filled out the information about me and asked to register to take the test. I crossed my fingers and whispered a little prayer that I would qualify for the test. I would have to wait for a response from the college before I could do anything else. In the interim, I began to talk more with Vickie about her experiences in getting into the college. She was filled with lots of information about the happenings that occurred at the school and the more she talked about them, the more I wanted to go to school. She mentioned that many students lived in dormitories. She painted the picture of life in the dormitories as almost one big party. She talked of the vast number of men students that would be attending the school at the same time, and how many of them would be attending the parties. I could hardly comprehend such an atmosphere. But, my eagerness to join this group of young people was enhanced to the maximum height as she continued to extol the virtues of going away to college.

In early July, I received a letter from the college saying that, after they had looked at the transcript of my high school grades, I was definitely qualified to take the test for a full scholarship to the school. My only dilemma now was how was I going to get to Evansville to take the test? It was evident that I needed to inform Mother and Dad that I had been accepted to take the test.

That night at dinner, I began to tell them about the opportunity to take the test for a scholarship that had been offered to me. Dad was not a bit happy. He saw no need for me to get any further education. He reinforced Mother's opinion that I should just find a man in Otwell, get married, settle down, and raise a family like every other young woman. However, Mother came to my defense and began to question me about what I would be doing at the school. I stoically withheld the information about the parties that Vickie had described to me. I was certain that the idea of partying was not an acceptable behavior for a serious student trying to get an education. After a long discussion among the three of us, my parents finally decided to allow me to take the test for the scholarship. Dad agreed to take me to the school on the morning of the test, and stay in Evansville until the test was over. Mother chimed in to say that she would accompany him on the trip, and that the two of them would see the sights of the city while they were there. I could hardly believe that this was really happening to me.

Chapter 15

Taking the test was my first experience in what life might be like somewhere other than Otwell, Indiana. I passed the test with flying colors, although I found some of the questions quite strange. I was so glad that I had spent part of my summer at the library in Jasper reading about the war. My interest in the war gave me the insight that I needed to easily answer any questions pertaining to the foreign countries. Summer was coming to an end, and my life could soon change.

It was time to travel to Evansville in order to register for classes at Evansville College. I had been given a room in the dormitory of the school. We packed up the things that we thought that we would need to survive for the coming year. Mother had been making sheets and pillow cases for several weeks so that I would have enough to use until Thanksgiving. Vickie's mother had been doing the same. We packed towels and bedding, blankets, book cases, and trunks full of clothes. We wanted to make sure that we had everything that we could possibly need for the coming semester. It would be winter soon, and I would need winter clothes too. Needless to say my trunk was bulging at the hinges with the things that I was convinced that I couldn't live without for one year.

My trunk was so full of clothing that Dad was hardly able to load it into the wagon. Mother continued to tell me that I was taking all the wrong clothing, but I would not hear of leaving anything behind. My vow to myself was that I would get rid of all those old clothes once that I got on campus and could see what the other girls were wearing. I knew how to sew some things, so I could probably re-work some of my wardrobe into something that was more fashionable. At least, that is the story that I told myself.

Just prior to our leaving for school, Vickie's father purchased a Model T. Ford. He agreed to take us both to school in his car. Dad was delighted that he didn't have to negotiate his wagon and team around Evansville with all the street cars and trolley tracks. He knew that sometimes horses were 'spooked' by the sound of the 'horseless carriages' or the trolleys.

On Tuesday, we loaded our personal belongings in the back seat, leaving room for us to ride, and strapped the trunks on the back of the car. Vickie's mother had prepared a picnic lunch for us to enjoy on the trip. It was like a dream come true, this excursion into another world for two girls from Otwell. The future for us was unknown and unpredictable. It was to offer great consequences for each of us.

Chapter 16

We arrived on campus shortly after 4:00 P.M. Our room in the dormitory was on the second floor. It took us about two hours to unload all our belongings and get them carried up to our room. While we were busily trying to get our possessions into our room, I noticed a few young men walking around on the campus. It was so exciting to see young men dressed in nice clothing instead of bib overalls. I wanted to speak to each of them, but the chore at hand was occupying our time.

While Vickie's father was struggling to get the trunks up the stairs, a nice looking young man came to our rescue and offered his assistance. When all of the bags had been carried up the stairway to our room, the young man introduced himself as Wayne Hallert. He was a sophomore at the school and lived on campus also. He was originally from Washington, Indiana, which was a town not far from Otwell. He spoke kindly to Vickie's father and assured him that he would help us if either of us needed someone. He shook hands with her father and casually walked away. I was completely enamored with the young man. When I turned to check on Vickie, I saw that she was looking longingly after Wayne. I smiled to myself that she probably had first 'dibs' on him since it was her father that he was assisting. I was certain that he had friends or that we might find other men on campus. It appeared to me that they were everywhere. Surely we were in for a good time.

Chapter 17

Vickie and I rambled across the campus of Evansville College. It seemed so big and overwhelming. We met many other students as we ambled along; some were friendly and some simply went about their own business. We knew that classes were scheduled to begin the following Monday but we needed to know where we would be going for each class. However, daylight was beginning to fade, and we knew that the first place that we needed to find was the dining hall. Our lunch was getting low and we were anxious to see what we would have to eat for our dinner.

When we arrived on campus, the Registrar had given us a map that we could use to find our way around to the various buildings. When we returned to our room, we found the map under a stack of other papers and information. Studying the map, we discovered that the dining hall was at the other end of the campus and dinner was at 6:00 P.M. It was nearly that time while we were looking at the map. I turned to Vickie and said that I was on my way to eat. I did not intend to miss this meal. The two of us took off running the length of three large buildings trying to get to the dining hall before they closed for the evening. In our haste to beat the clock, we encountered three young men hurrying in the same direction. They asked why we were in such a big rush, to which we explained that we were on our way to the dining hall. "I hate to tell you girls, but the dining hall is the other direction," said one. "Some one played a trick on the campus and turned the sign around. You need to run the other way."

Another one of the young men stepped up and agreed to help us find the dining hall, and introduced him self as "Perry Stratford". "I will go with you until you find your way. Where do you live on campus?" he asked.

We replied in unison that we lived in the big red brick building to the East of where we were running. "That is the Monon Hall," he replied. "You will need to know the name of your building or you will be lost all the time."

About the time that he had finished admonishing us for not knowing where we lived, we reached the dining hall. He entered with us. We all quickly got in line to get a tray for food. We had to show our identification card to be able to purchase the food for our dinner. After we had received our portion of food, we found a table and Perry joined us.

GEORGE JACKSON
January 2, 1900
Chapter 18

George rode his horse as hard as he could. He wanted to leave his past behind him. He continued trying to make his horse run faster. He wasn't sure where he was going; he only knew that he wanted to get away from Otwell, Indiana, and from the life he had lived there. The wind was whipping against his face and snow had begun to fall again, making his trip even more miserable.

He just kept thinking that what he had done was wrong. He knew that Lula would not want him to give their baby away. But, he had already done that dastardly deed, and he had to try getting it out of his mind. He had done what he could for her; he had given the baby her name. Surely Lula would understand that he had done that for her. Would God forgive him? He kept trying to tell himself that he had no other choice. For now, he had to get away, far enough away that he could forget! Where was he going? He didn't know the answer to that? He had never been anywhere beyond Otwell, Jasper, and the other small towns around where he had lived.

George had gone to school at the same school where his father had attended. When he was younger, his father was his teacher. After he had finished elementary school, high school in Otwell had been an interesting experience for one year; then his father had been killed, and he could no longer attend school. He was able to read and write, but had very few other skills. He knew that he could hunt and fish enough to survive on his own. But how could he make a living? All of these queries that were rolling around in his mind helped him to forget the last 24 hours.

It was getting dark and he knew the horse needed a rest. He looked for a place where he might bed down for the night. He saw an old barn in the distance off on his right. Could he hole up in there for the night, he wondered? If a farmer came by and found him, he wouldn't object to his sleeping in a barn with his horse, would he? George had never needed to ask for help before now, but he felt so desperately alone and helpless.

He dismounted his horse and led her inside the barn for shelter. She seemed quite appreciative and shook the snow off her body as they entered the rickety structure. George wasn't sure if anyone had been in this barn in years except for rats and snakes. He knew the snakes were gone for the winter, but he wasn't sure about the rats. He found an old pitchfork hanging on the wall and used it to scrape some straw together for him and his horse to sleep on. His horse would provide the warmth for him until they could do better. He pulled a blanket from his knapsack and tried to cover himself with it, but it smelled just like Lula's perfume.

He folded it and put it back where he found it. He couldn't bear to think about her now. He nestled down next to the horse's back and fell asleep instantly. He didn't realize that it was the first good night's sleep that he had had in several days.

Chapter 19

George Jackson knew that he had to find work soon. He wasn't a slacker; he had always worked very hard on the farm, trying to make a living for Lula. He had worked on his father's farm since he was a small boy, so he knew that farming was hard work. However, he wanted to do something different, but he didn't know what it might be or where to look. When he had awakened early in the morning he realized that he had no home, but no responsibilities. He had given his home and farm to the neighbor in exchange for a good life for his baby daughter. Now, he had only one thing to consider, himself.

He straightened out the barn where he had slept for one night, saddled his horse, and rode off toward town hoping to find something to eat and then search for a job.

He saw a sign along the road that said Vincennes. He knew very little about what Vincennes would have to offer, but it appeared to be bigger than Otwell and Jasper both. He felt that it might hold an opportunity for him. He stopped in a small grocery store and asked for directions to a diner or café where he could get a meal. He was directed on down the road to a small café where a sign stated, "breakfast - 2 bits". George was certain that the price was right, and he might just eat two of those meals at that price.

While he was dining on the sumptuous breakfast,

he asked some of the other men in the diner where he might find a job. Some of the men only knew about farm work. George cringed at the thought of working on a farm again. However, one man mentioned that they were hiring down by the river, if he wanted to help load barges for the river traffic. As he was leaving the café to go to the river, a young man approached him and asked to speak to him privately. He took him aside and told him about the railroad that was beginning to run through Vincennes. It was part of the main line running from Chicago to Evansville, carrying freight from one city to another. The man wasn't sure how much farther to the south the train went but he knew that it stopped in Evansville. There were also passenger cars on the line for influential people who needed to travel. It made a regular stop in Vincennes on its way between the two cities. The man related that there might be an opening for a job on the train, if he was willing to start work as a fireman on the engine. It would be a hard and hot job shoveling coal into the coal burner that generated steam for the engine. But, if a man worked hard, he could eventually work his way into a better job.

George could hardly believe what he was hearing. He understood hard work and he was willing to do anything to earn a good living. He took the information that he needed to apply to the railroad company and he headed down to the stationhouse to find the man whom he needed to see.

When George rode up to the stationhouse, he was amazed at the size of the train's engine. He looked at it for a long time, wondering just how he could ever do the job that they might be offering. He went inside the building, still thinking about the size of that engine, where he met the man who appeared to be in charge of the hiring and firing of new employees. George introduced himself and mentioned that he had talked with someone at the café earlier in the day about a possible job on the train. When the man stood up, he seemed young and vibrant as he introduced himself as James Bertram, the engineer on the train sitting on the rails right outside. George was mystified. He hardly knew one position from another, so he began asking some questions. James was quite patient with him and explained that there were many opportunities with the railroad; some men helped to lay the rails that the train ran on, and some men helped the train to run. The engineer was the man in charge of the train's running properly. It was the top position that had to be earned through many years of service. A conductor handled the patrons on the passenger train. And, he went on to explain several other positions that were needed for the train to run properly. George was so intrigued by all the information about running a train that he almost forgot the reason why he was there. He wanted to apply for a job.

James took him in the office and gave him a sheet of paper to complete so that he could be considered for a job. George looked at the paper and realized that the first line asked for his address. He had none. He went on to read the paper and noticed that it stated that he would be traveling between Evansville and Terre Haute. The pay for his work was to be $.75 per hour of work not including layover time at any of the depots. He noted at the very end, that the railroad company would pay $.25 per night if the train was detained in any town overnight because of a breakdown.

George signed his name at the bottom and left the address blank. He turned to James and told him that he would be back the next morning to fill in the address line since he had just arrived in Vincennes.

He left the train station and went down to the main street looking for a boarding house. When he arrived at the big white house on the corner, he knocked gently. He felt sure that he could get a room there which would give him an address to put on his job application.

A portly woman answered his knock on the door. She gazed at the rather unsightly man standing before her and questioned why he was there. "I need a room," George said.

"Are you a transient?" she asked.

"No ma'am," he replied. "I have applied for a job with the railroad, and I need an address in Vincennes. Do you have a room that I can rent?"

"I am not sure," she answered. "Can you tell me how long you will be staying?"

"I plan to stay a long time," he stated. "I am in need

of a home."

Mrs. Thomas stepped aside and motioned for him to come inside. "Tell me a little about yourself," she said.

George settled into a large overstuffed chair and began to tell Mrs. Thomas that he had been traveling a long time to begin a new life. He mentioned that his wife had died, but he withheld the information about his baby daughter. He wasn't ready to tell that part yet. Then he realized that he hadn't had a bath or shaved for more than a week. "I must look like a ragged old man," he offered as an explanation for his looks.

"Well, yes," Mrs. Thomas replied, "you do look a bit worse for wear. Tell me, can you pay for room and board if I allow you to stay?"

"I have enough money to pay for a few weeks and then I will have a salary from the railroad."

"You may have the upstairs bedroom. I require that no women be brought into the room. Any courting will be done in the parlor. Lights must be out at 11:00 p.m., meals are served in the dining room at 6:30 a.m., 12:00 noon, and 6:00 p.m. If you are late, you will miss your meals. Are these rules acceptable?"

"Oh, yes, Mrs. Thomas, they are more than acceptable. I am so grateful for a bed to sleep in and a meal on the table." He reached into his pocket and paid for the room for two weeks. He took his horse around to the stable and gave her some hay while he went inside to get a bath and shave. He wanted to look like a human being again.

After a good night's sleep, two good meals and the promise of a job, George Jackson began leaving his troubles behind him, at least for the time being.

Chapter 20

George went into the railroad office to leave his address on the paper that he had signed the day before. He mentioned to James that he had acquired a room at the local boarding house on 6th St. James laughed and told him that many of the railroad men had stayed at that house. Mrs. Thomas was one great cook, he added.

James gave him the necessary information that he would need to begin the job as fireman. He could begin the next day if he wanted to report for work at 7:00 a.m. George shook his hand and stated that he would be there right on time.

George walked out of the office, smiling as he mounted up on his faithful roan steed. He wondered where this job would take him. He had never been on a train and now he was going to be working on one. How strange, he thought. Then his thoughts turned to Lilli. He wondered if she was OK. As her image came into his mind, he felt tears coming into his eyes. He rode his horse to the end of the street before he could stop the tears from flowing. He really missed seeing his baby. Someday, he would, he vowed.

Chapter 21

George began working for the railroad. The name of the train line was the Chicago and Eastern Illinois or C&EI as it was commonly called. His first few days were very demanding. He wanted to do a good job so he tried to listen carefully to what the man in charge was telling him. He was told that there would be several stops along the road from Chicago to Evansville. Then the train would take a track to the Illinois side and go back to Chicago through Illinois. He hardly understood anything about a railroad track. He knew that there was a train that ran near Otwell, but he had never been on a train in his life. He had never been to Illinois, either, and he wondered if it were any different than Indiana. When his shift on the train was over for the day, he realized that he was in Evansville. He got off the train but soon got back on because it was dark and he didn't know where to go in a strange city. He asked the engineer if he could sleep on the train. The engineer smiled and told him that he should go with him to the hotel where he was staying and he could get a room for the night there. George agreed to follow him, taking his advice.

After a good night's sleep, George and the engineer went back to the stationhouse to wait for the train to come into the yard for that day's journey. It would be a trip through Illinois and George could hardly wait for this adventure.

As the train sped through the countryside of Illinois, George could see that it looked very much like Indiana. There were large farms along the railroad bed, and he knew that the farmers would be working very hard to till all that land. Some of the areas had small towns where the train would stop and take on water and more passengers. He watched as the men and women boarded the train to go wherever it would take them. He was so fascinated by how they were dressed and the baggage that they took with them. He had never seen women dressed so fine or men with bowler hats and canes. It was obviously a life that George had never experienced. He wondered if he would ever be able to dress like that. Just where would these men be going in such a fine costume? And where would the women get the finery that they were wearing? Their clothing did not look like it had been made in the kitchen or bedroom like all the women in Otwell. Was it wrong of him to think about other women? Lula would want him to find another woman to take care of him, wouldn't she? Would he ever live such a life that he was personally witnessing? Right now, the only woman in his life was Mrs. Thomas. She was a rather plump woman, and probably twenty years older than he. However, she appeared to be clean and she always smelled like 'lilies of the valley'. He loved that fragrance. Maybe he should consider what was available to him at the moment.

Chapter 22

George worked on the train, shoveled coal in the firebox, helped to guide the water hose into the boiler, and all the other chores that the engineer gave him to do as the train sped toward Chicago. He loved his job although it was hot and dirty. He found it fascinating and educational as he the train hurried toward its destination. He knew that when he got to Chicago, the train would go into the roundhouse and turn completely around on the circular tract, a feat that completely mystified him. Then, they would reconnect the train cars and head down the Indiana side of the tracks. His first turnaround on the train had been so interesting that he was overflowing with questions. He wanted to hurry home and be able to share his stories with Mrs. Thomas, if she was interested in hearing them.

George stayed with the C&EI railroad company for several years. He became quite adept at doing most of the jobs required. He still reveled at the scenes that he witnessed as the trains sped across the plains. He watched as the farmers' planted corn and wheat, and then watched as they harvested their crops in the fall. He could relate to them as they struggled to beat the weather. Those experiences took him back to his life in Otwell. They were trying to make a living for their families, just as he had done when Lula was alive.

George always returned to Mrs. Thomas' boarding house when he completed his run. He handled many small chores for her around her home. One year, in the spring, he began to paint her house. He assured her that it might take a few weeks for him to complete the job, but she laughed and told him that she would never be able to get it done if he didn't do it.

However, George had other feelings. He had been a widower for several years. He longed for the comfort of a woman. He had been true to Lula and he missed her very much but he had laid her in the cold ground in the cemetery in Otwell a long time ago. Now he was a man with passion in his heart. He had watched Mrs. Thomas in her daily routine and he wondered just what she would be like as a wife. He loved the odor that she had about her. It seemed like it was spring flowers. He observed her as she went about her morning routine, she had a lovely way about her before she dressed in her street clothes. He envisioned what she might look like without her filmy negligee. Then, he would chastise himself for having thoughts about her like that. She was at least 20 years older than he. She would certainly not be interested in him. She considered him her son, or so he thought.

Mrs. Thomas watched George as he went about his regular routine. He was gone on the train for many days and would return home at different hours on different days. She waited anxiously for him to return and longed for his stories about what he had seen this time on his trips. She could feel a stirring in her heart for this fine young man, but she knew he was young enough to be her son. She wondered why she was so enamored with him. Maybe she was just lonely. But, she had not had these feeling for several years. However, she tried to quell her feelings for him since she didn't think they would be reciprocated. Each time he was around her, she wanted to reach out to him, but she refrained from touching him. What would he think of her? And, if she moved toward him first, he might be offended and then move out of her home. She would lose him completely. That thought gave her cold chills. She didn't want to lose him at all. She preferred to stay her distance and dream about cozy nights with him in her bed.

George continued to work on the train and return to Mrs. Thomas' home when his shift was over. He anxiously awaited his time with her. He often wanted to call her by name, but he maintained his distance and the formality of calling her Mrs. Thomas. But, he never stopped thinking about her while he was gone.

When he got off his shift on Friday evening, he hurried home to what he hoped was a fine meal and an evening with Mrs. Thomas. "On this Friday, I will approach the subject," he thought, "and I will let the chips fall where they may. If she is offended, I will find another place to live and start over with my life. But, if she is amenable to my advances, I will explain how I feel about her," he continued telling himself.

He walked up on the porch, reached for the door handle and hurried inside. He would make a small gesture tonight. If she resisted his advance then he would know that she was not interested. If she didn't shy away, then he would feel comforted. He could only wait and see what her reaction would be. Mrs. Thomas was busy in the kitchen when he came into the house. He could smell her wonderful pot roast cooking on the stove. He walked up behind her and put his hands around her waist, leaning in to nuzzle her hair. She turned around and looked him in the eye. He slowly kissed her on the cheek. To his surprise, she put her arms around him and hid her face in his shoulder cavity. "I have waited a long time for this," she said. "We have many things to talk about tonight."

George reached out and took Mrs. Thomas' hand and led her to the master bedroom, leaving the enticing pot roast on the stove to be savored later. Right now, he was going to bring to fruition the thoughts that he had been having for quite some time. He could see that she was quite amenable to his advances. Soon he would be able to cuddle and make love to the woman who had come into his life a few years ago, and who had seen to his every domestic need. Now, he was exploring his physical needs.

George had not expected such a wonderful experience. He reflected on the idea that she was old enough to be his mother, but the past hour convinced him that she was young at heart and receptive to his amorous advances. During the course of exploring each other, she had whispered to him that he should call her Barbara Ann.

Chapter 23

Each evening when George returned from work, he began reading the local newspaper that Barbara had delivered to the house. He read with interest the story of the massive unemployment in America. He had noticed, as the train was rambling across the prairie in Illinois that many of the stores were boarded up and businesses seemed to be closed. He also noted that there were long lines in some of the larger cities outside churches. One of his fellow workers on the train explained that these were 'bread lines'. George could hardly imagine the plight of those people who had to literally beg for their food, and then he remembered when he was sleeping in barns and eating what he could find from the hands of generous strangers. How could he have forgotten so soon? His friend explained that the country was heading toward a depression. It seemed to George that the entire country was in deep trouble with difficult situations on all fronts. He certainly didn't understand what it all meant. And he wondered if his baby girl was getting enough to eat.

He could hardly wait to discuss all these problems with Barbara when he was home in the evening. She seemed remarkably informed on the situation of the country and she patiently explained all the details to George. She listened to the radio daily and could explain to him situations as they happened. A new president, Franklin Delano Roosevelt had just been elected and it was his intention to help the country recover from the Great Depression.

George was grateful that he had a good job and didn't really want to lose his security. He loved what he was doing and he felt that there was opportunity for him to go on beyond fireman on the railroad and eventually become the conductor. He looked forward to the day when he could meet and greet the passengers as they boarded the train to go somewhere. He had the best job that he could have ever hoped for, and he was convinced that people in Otwell would never believe that he had made such drastic changes in his life.

While he was considering his future, suddenly, he had an old feeling. He wondered where Lilli was and if he would ever be able to see her again. He knew that she was growing up and probably married with her own family. He did long to see her, just one more time. He wanted to tell her why he felt that he had to leave her. He had kept his secret to himself all of the years since he left Otwell. No one knew that he was once a family man. No one had ever asked.

BACK TO LILLI
Chapter 24

Lilli and Vickie settled into their dorm room and began to talk about all the things that they expected to be doing while they were in college. Particularly of interest to them was the fact that they were going to be meeting some young men that were not from the Otwell area. From their experience the night before, when they had been lost on their way to the cafeteria, the two girls decided that they should take some time and walk around the campus as part of settling in. They needed to be able to find their classrooms without stumbling around looking like they were fresh from the country.

The two girls reviewed their wardrobes and decided that some of their clothing was typical of farm girls. They did not want to reveal that they were 'country-bumpkins'. Lilli had been going to the library in Jasper and perusing the magazines there, trying to understand what the latest styles might be. She noticed that skirts were long and fitted to the body. It appeared that large billowing clothing was going out of style. She also discovered that the skirts were much shorter; in fact, they seemed to allow about 7 or 8 inches of the woman's leg to show. Shoes were not the high top style that the girls had been wearing to high school, but they were buttoned around the ankle. Lilli and Vickie decided that they would visit a local library to study just what would be acceptable for them to wear now that they were going to be living in the 'city'. Although, they could see what the other girls were wearing, they did not want to be copy-cats. They hoped to be the trend-setters for the other girls to follow.

There were still two days before classes were to begin, so it gave the girls a little time to develop their plan of action. Early the next morning the two girls took off to find the nearest library. They were relieved to find that it was only about 3 blocks away. As they walked up the steps to the large brick building, Lilli stated that it was much larger than the Jasper Library and she wondered if it were because it was in Evansville, or was it that this city had more money to build a library. She looked up to see a large embossed name scrawled across the façade of the library, stating that it was a "Carnegie Library". She knew from the information that she had learned in school that Andrew Carnegie had donated money to build a great number of libraries across the United States. She was so impressed to find that there was one of his libraries where she could visit. As Vickie slowed her pace, Lilli began to fill her in on the information about Carnegie that she could remember from the news Father had talked about while they were eating dinner. As the two girls entered the large impressive building it still smelled new to them. It apparently had been built within the last year or so. But, it was stocked with more books than the girls could imagine.

The two girls spoke to the librarian and told her that they wanted to look at some magazines on fashion as well as the latest rotogravures. Lilli remembered that the librarian in Jasper had introduced her to the rotogravures, which were magazines published by the fashion houses in New York. She had spent many hours perusing them while visiting in Jasper.

While Vickie had never noticed these publications before, she and Lilli spent most of the morning looking at the newest fashions. It appeared that the styles changed sometime around 1918, shortly after World War I had ended. When the soldiers who had been fighting the war in Europe, returned home to their families, they discovered that women had dropped the old long dresses and high top work shoes for slimmer and shorter dresses. Many of the men did not like the idea that their wives legs would be showing and insisted that their wives continue the same style of dress that their mothers had worn. But that certainly was not what the two girls wanted to wear. They wanted to be more fashionable than their mothers had been.

Lilli and Vickie continued their quest for ideas of how fashionable women of the 20's were going to look. They hurried back to their dorm room and began to re-fashion their entire wardrobes. The girls also noticed that the hats adorned with large flowers and feathers were gone too. The hats of this day were tight fitting to the head covering most of the very short hair. What a revolution, the two girls thought. They were sure that they could not return to Otwell in their new wardrobe or they would be laughed out of town. However, in Evansville, Indiana, they were going to be very fashionable as long as they could continue to visit the library and sew reasonably well.

It was nearly daylight when the two girls were satisfied that they had enough stylish clothes to attend classes without being thought of as 'folks from the country'. They were now well prepared to be 'city girls'. While they may have been dressed to the 'nines', there were still many things the girls would be learning in the very near future.

Chapter 25

Classes began and the two girls were well on their way to getting the long awaited education. Their schedule was quite hectic and most of their evenings were occupied with homework. Food at the cafeteria was not like what they were used to eating at home, but it was plentiful and tasty. After the girls were acclimated to early morning classes, and late lunches, they began to talk to other students about outside activities. They heard other girls discussing parties held by one of the sororities. Neither girl even knew what a sorority was and had no idea of how to be invited to one of their parties.

When Friday evening came, both girls dressed in what they considered their finest outfit and simply went to the building where the most noise was coming from, to see what was going on. As they went inside the building they were stopped at the door by another girl. She questioned the two about their membership in the sorority. Of course, neither Lilli nor Vickie were members, but the girl at the door assured them that they could become members by applying. But, for this night, they were invited to stay for the party as visitors,

Vickie and Lilli had never been to such a party. The students were all dancing to a rather wild sort of dance that the two girls had never seen before. Someone told them it was called "The Charleston". One of the young men took Lilli by the hand and agreed to teach her how to do it. Before long, both of the young women were engrossed in doing this new dance and mingling with the other young men at the party. When the clock struck eleven o'clock, Vickie and Lilli had to hurry out of the party to be able to get back to their dorm before the curfew and 'lights-out' was sounded. As the girls dragged their weary bodies' home, they were worn out from dancing with all the men that were at the party. And their feet were aching from learning the new steps to the 'Charleston'. Their conversation was slight since neither of them had much energy for conversation. There would be time for talking the next day, but for tonight, they fell into their beds and slept from sheer exhaustion. They were almost giddy with excitement at the new turn of events in their life.

Chapter 26

School work at Evansville College now took on a different meaning. There was work in the classroom to complete, but there were activities on campus, the likes of which, neither girl had ever experienced. Life in Otwell became a blur. Nothing like this action had ever taken place in their home town. If it had, it had not included Lilli or Vickie. They were oblivious of what was going on at home; in fact, it never crossed their mind.

They both applied to join the sorority called Delta Theta Phi. The girls had no idea what all that meant, but it was explained that it was an ancient Greek name that referred to a specific group of girls who would pledge to remain faithful to their 'sisters' in the sorority. The fees were not too high for their membership, and both girls were able to save the membership dues out of the stipend that had been given to them by the school. Although the membership supposedly offered a lot of things for the girls, the only thing that really interested them was the parties and intermingling with the men on campus who belonged to Fraternities. As was explained to them, the fraternities were the same as sororities except that only men could be members. Vickie and Lilli had no interest in any explanation, just the association of the two groups. The two girls looked forward to the weekends when the parties would usually begin around 7:00 in the evening on Friday and continued until the wee hours of the morning on Sunday.

Lilli and Vickie were learning to dance every new dance step that they saw someone else doing at the parties. And they were also learning a lot of other things, too.

The girls were learning about prohibition, or the banning of the sale of alcohol. However, that didn't deter the young people on campus from drinking. In fact, the term "bathtub gin" was so popular, that most of the students had as much alcohol as they could consume although it was not legal. Someone always knew how to get all the 'booze' that the young students could drink. The consumption of alcohol seemed to be the primary reason for partying at the weekend events. Some of the students would go on picnics down by the banks of the Ohio River which flowed by the city, but most of them preferred the privacy of the fraternity or sorority houses. Soon, the two girls found that there really were other things happening at the school. During some of the parties held at the sorority houses, there had been men involved.

Lilli discovered that sometimes girls had smuggled a young man and booze up to their room. Soon Lilli was doing the same thing. She had met a man with whom she was sure she was in love with at one of the dances. Grayson Parton was a very handsome young man. He was very tall and quite a dapper dresser. He always looked his best at the parties, and he seemed to have unlimited funds for buying their liquor. Lilli invited Grayson up to her room with the ruse that she had some questions about her most recent homework. He cheerfully brought his silver flask filled with whiskey with him and the two of them sat on the bed sharing the contents of the flask. Soon, Grayson was making passionate love to Lilli and she was enjoying every minute of it. He told her how he had fallen in love with her over the past months that they had been attending the parties. He stroked her hair and whispered things in her ear that she loved to hear. Soon, the two of them were seen together all over the campus. Lilli was, indeed, in love. Each time that Grayson would stop by her room, she would send Vickie on her way out of the room so that she and Grayson could be alone. At the same time, Vickie was enjoying the company of a young man from another fraternity. Vickie had met the man of her dreams at a party on the beach one night. His name was Tom Howard. It wasn't long until Vickie was bringing him to her room, too, on a regular basis. He was not a very handsome man, but appeared to have unlimited funds. His father owned a hardware store in Evansville and had sent his son to college to get an education. The young man had already been quite a problem for his father, having taken funds from the cash register on two separate occasions. Tom appeared to lie when it would have been easier to tell the truth, but Vickie appeared to be blinded by his faults. She was madly and passionately in love with him. Her conversations during the day were of nothing else except Tom Howard. She was sure that he would marry her and take her away from Otwell. Unfortunately Tom Howard was not a very honorable man. He was courting another girl on campus at the same time that he was enjoying the company of Vickie. His father had bought him a car so he was able to take either of the girls on trips to Henderson or Vincennes and even into Illinois for the weekend. When he was with the other girl, he continued to tell Vickie that he was working in his father's store. Since Vickie had no transportation, she couldn't verify his story, but she would not have questioned him anyway. She was so in love with him that she trusted his every move.

Lilli was also enjoying Grayson and found him to be a perfect gentleman. He too had a car, and would take Lilli on trips throughout the countryside on Sunday afternoon. He told her his life's story which involved his growing up in a town to the west called Mt. Vernon. His family had owned a large farm in Posey County where they raised beef cattle. They also had many acres that they planted in soybeans and corn which they sold at the local mill. Grayson did not consider his family wealthy, but they seemed to be able to afford some of the luxuries of life that Lilli had never imagined having. Her father was a farmer, but he never seemed to be successful enough to give the family many things from 'the good life'. Her family had always seemed to live from year to year on the bare minimum of money.

Lilli had attended church all her formative years and felt an obligation to resume her church attendance. Grayson willingly introduced her to the chapel on campus and the two of them began to attend together. Their Saturday night parties had to be cut short so that they would be sober on Sunday morning. Lilli could hardly wait for church to be over so that she and Grayson could go somewhere and share what was in his silver flask. She never realized how much she was becoming dependant on a 'drink'. It never occurred to her that her drinking was an addiction. Grayson was not judgmental of her; however, he would sometimes tell her that the flask was empty to keep her from having another drink. Always after their drinking sprees, they would make passionate love if they were in a location that afforded them privacy.

Chapter 27

School came easy to Lilli. She seemed to be above average when it came to understanding what the professors were trying to teach. She was convinced that she would make a great teacher herself someday. As her school years were winding down, she thought back to her life in Otwell. It had been several years since she had been involved in anything that had happened in her home town. She had rarely made the trip back to see the Hortons. She did not have a car and neither did her family. She had been able to ride back home with Vickie's parents when they came to get her for a visit with them. Lilli had soon found out that she did not have much in common with her own family. Their lives seemed to evolve around the family farm and very little more. She never celebrated her birthday with them, and her heritage was never mentioned. She still had that unanswered question lingering in her subconscious. Lilli found their conversations boring and uninteresting, and she never shared with them the things that were taking place on campus. When she asked about what Mother had seen or heard while shopping in Jasper, she was always told that she saw no one that she knew there. Lilli found herself anxiously awaiting the car that would take her back to school and her life at the college. And, more than ever, she missed Grayson. Although he had visited her during the summer at her home in Otwell, she missed their private times. When she introduced him to her parents, they were cordial to him. He put forth a good front for them and they were pleased at their daughter's choice in men.

Once, when Grayson was visiting, she took him to a park in Jasper and they were able to share his silver flask, but they were not able to have a sexual encounter. Lilli laughed that she was unable to have sex in her own home town. Some day, that will change, she mused. Until then, she really longed for her return to classes at school.

When Lilli's senior year began, she wondered how she would be able to use her college degree. She would be equipped to teach school, but somehow that did not interest her. She wasn't sure what else she could do with the 'almighty piece of paper' called a diploma from college.

Graduation was only one month away. Lilli knew that she needed to be applying for a job at some local school. She wasn't sure how to do that, but Evansville College had a placement department that assisted graduating students in finding employment after graduation. She visited the office and the lady assured her that her grades were so good that she would easily be able to get a job at a nearby school. Lilli would have to find an apartment near the school where she would be teaching since she still did not have a car. Of course, her thoughts turned to Grayson. If he would ask her to marry him, perhaps she would be able to learn to drive his car. Not many women drove cars in 1923. Lilli wanted to be one of those few. She would ask Grayson to teach her how to drive his car.

Grayson did not mind teaching her how to drive his car, but he needed to talk with her about her drinking. He did not want to teach her how to drive if she was going to drink the amount of alcohol that he had witnessed her drinking lately. He would bring the subject up and see what her reaction turned out to be.

Vickie was on a whirlwind. She was so in love with Tom that she wanted to spend most of her time with him. Her schoolwork was falling behind. Tom had already stopped attending classes but had not told his father that he was through with Evansville College. His father was giving him a weekly allowance and he knew if he told his father that he had quit school, the money would stop. Only a fool would break up the money trail, he thought. He promised to tell him later. Vickie was also cutting classes and it looked as if she would not have enough credits to graduate. Lilli tried to coach her and help her with her schoolwork so that she could graduate, but Vickie was totally disinterested. All she wanted was Tom Howard and she had no idea that another girl also wanted him. Tom was dividing his time between Vickie and another girl who was a student at the College but lived off campus. Tom could go to her house and spend the night when her parents weren't home. Then he would come back to see Vickie the very next night.

Lilli and Grayson had taken a picnic lunch to the

river one Saturday afternoon. Who should they see at the beach but Tom Howard romancing the other girl? Lilli had to look twice to make sure that what she was seeing was the real thing. Lilli was certain that the man was Tom Howard and she didn't recognize the other girl. But she did witness the two of them going off into the woods which bordered the beach where they were all having their picnic. When they came out of the woods, Tom was rearranging his clothes and it seemed quite obvious what had been happening in the woods.

Lilli tried to talk to Grayson about the situation, but he calmly stated that it wasn't any of her business. If Vickie was fooled by Tom, it was because she wasn't paying much attention. Everyone who knew Tom Howard, knew that he was 'no-good' and that he would only take Vickie for a ride.

While Lilli and Grayson were at the beach for their picnic, he asked her what her plans were after graduation. She mentioned that she probably would get a job teaching at a nearby school. He mentioned that he might stay on at the school and get another degree. He really didn't want to go home to the farm, and he wasn't sure that he wanted to teach. He had been thinking about medical school. Evansville did not have a medical school, which meant that he would have to move out of town if he chose to become a doctor. Lilli cringed. She did not like the idea of him leaving Evansville; at least not without her. She fell silent and did not respond to his idea. Suddenly he turned to her and asked what she thought.

"I really don't want you to leave Evansville," she replied.

"I would not be leaving you."

"If you moved away to go to medical school, you would be leaving me."

"Maybe I would just take you with me."

Lilli fell stone still. Had Grayson just proposed to her? Could she get a job teaching somewhere else in Indiana? She hardly knew how to respond.

"Am I to take this as a proposal," she asked.

"I am not very good at this, but yes, I guess I was sorta proposing."

"Sorta proposing, explain that."

Grayson leaned closer to her and placed his hands on her face, turning it to look in his eyes. "Lilli, he said, I've made no secret that I have fallen in love with you. I must make my decision based on what my parents say. They can afford to send me on to medical school, but I don't know if they are willing. They have always wanted me to get some sort of agricultural degree, but it is not my interest. I think I would like to become a doctor. If we could manage to fit our love into my future plans, then that would be great for both of us."

Lilli thought about what he was saying. It didn't seem to be a passionate proposal like she had dreamed of in her childlike dreams. She wanted the young man to fall to his knees and whisper how he would vow to love her forever. Now, Grayson was saying that he loved her, but it would depend on how his plans would work out and if he could go to medical school. Lilli longed for a silver flask to give her the courage that she needed to address this dilemma. "I love you very much, Grayson. I guess what I am saying is that I am willing to take a school teaching position here nearby and wait for you to finish medical school. If your parents approve of your plans, and they choose to help us, then I could get a job at almost any school in Indiana and begin teaching. That would help support us while you attended Med school."

Grayson leaned back on the blanket and breathed a sigh of relief. "I was so afraid that you would not understand my desire to become a doctor." He leaned over and kissed her tenderly and saw that the Tom left after their tryst in the bushes. He had left his date on the beach alone. Grayson realized at that moment that Tom Howard had probably recognized them and did not want to be seen. What a scoundrel he is, thought Grayson. I am sorry that I know him. And, I actually feel sorry for Vickie because she doesn't see Tom for who he really is.

Chapter 28

Lilli and Grayson returned to the campus in the early afternoon soon after their picnic was over. Lilli could still see Tom with the other girl on the beach. It made her uncomfortable to think about it. She wasn't sure if she should tell Vickie or if she should try to forget it. If she chose to tell her, Vickie probably would not believe the story. In fact, Lilli thought that Vickie would be angry with her and not share other secrets with her. She didn't want that to happen. Vickie was the only close friend that she had on campus. If she lost Vickie's friendship, she would really be alone. They had always shared so much of their time together.

On the coming Saturday night, there was a big fraternity party that the two girls were invited to attend. Several of the sorority sisters were also invited to attend, and Lilli knew that the 'bootleg' whiskey would flow freely. She longed for those parties and the activities that went on there. She loved the dancing and the partying atmosphere, even though Grayson always took her home when he was sure that she had been drinking too much.

When the party was in full force and the students were dancing to the music, the police raided the party and began arresting the persons in attendance. Several of the students managed to skip out the back door. Some even jumped from the windows, but the police were interested in the person who had furnished the liquor. They quickly grabbed Tom and placed him in handcuffs. There were several other students that were unable to escape and had been arrested by the police. Vickie tried to align herself with Tom, but she was pushed aside. The arresting officers wanted Tom and had apparently been trying to find him for quite some time.

Grayson took the two girls back to their dormitory and told them to stay inside for the rest of the weekend. He wanted to make sure that the story of the arrests, that was sure to make the newspaper, died down before they dared to go back out on campus. At that point, Lilli decided that she needed to make some changes in her life before something really bad happened to her.

Chapter 29

On Monday morning the two girls returned to their classes. Tom Howard was obviously absent. The girls remained silent about the activities of the weekend, but Grayson told them that Tom was still in jail. He related that his father had refused to pay his bail and that he might be sentenced to 30 days in jail. What the police wanted to know was where he got the liquor and Tom wasn't talking.

Grayson seemed to assume the role of 'father of the two girls', trying to watch over them to make sure that they didn't get into any more trouble at school. He related to them that the fraternity had been placed on probation at the school and that further parties were banned. Grayson chose to withdraw from the fraternity because he didn't think it would be good if he chose to become a doctor and his school records showed his membership in a probationary club. He was quite serious about his career and he knew that he should not be included in any questionable behavior. He was also concerned about Lilli and her drinking habits. He decided that he needed to talk to her about the subject and he vowed to himself that he would do just that, on their next date.

Tom Howard's parents were not very happy with him. He was certain to be get a sentence of 30 days or more in jail for his behavior at the party and the fact that he had supplied the liquor for the event. His parents relented and pled with the judge to be lenient with him. They assured the judge that they would see that he commit no further infractions of the law if they would set their wayward son free. Tom did not really want to be set free to the custody of his parents. He felt that he would get better treatment at the hands of fellow prisoners in the jail. However, the judge listened to his parents and sentenced him to probation in the custody of his mother and dad. They gathered their son and his meager possessions from the jail and headed for home. Tom's father began a long tirade about the behavior of Tom and his meaningless lifestyle. It was obvious to Tom that his parents meant business, this time. He was allowed to go back to school in order to complete his studies. He would have to pull his grades up to a passing level before the semester ended. He would also have to leave the fraternity and live at home where his parents could supervise his behavior. His allowance for his expenses was cut quite short, and he felt that he could not exist on the paltry amount that they were agreeing to give him. Tom was seething inside as his father was laying down the rules.

Tom instantly realized that this was not a workable solution. He would have to devise a method of getting out of the clutches of his father. Working in his father's hardware store was not his idea of a good job, anyway. He really didn't want to continue school if he couldn't be the 'party goer' that his reputation had earned him. He knew that he had to devise a plan of 'escape' for himself before it was too late.

Vickie mourned the fact that the partying that she had enjoyed with Tom was about to end. He shared with her the rules that his father had set for him and his discomfort with trying to live up to those standards. He assured her that he would come up with an alternative plan that he would execute and that she would be a part of it, whatever it turned out to be.

In the mean time, Vickie was experiencing some illness. She had a voracious appetite, but most of the food that she was eating was going straight through her. Lilli had advised her that she needed to stop drinking the 'bootleg' alcohol since it probably had many impurities in it. Lilli shared with her the facts that Grayson had given her about drinking. She, herself, had vowed to him that she would not be drinking that liquor any more. Now, she felt it was time to be a supporter of Vickie because she seemed to not be doing so well.

School was nearly out for the summer and the two girls would be going home to Otwell for the summer. However, Lilli noticed that Vickie was getting sicker every day. Now, it seemed that Vickie was vomiting each morning when she awakened. Nothing that Vickie would eat seemed to stay in her stomach until about 10:00 A.M. At that hour she appeared to be recovering and would do well until late in the evening. Her energy level was waning by dinner time and she became quite lethargic. When Lilli shared all these symptoms with Grayson, he began to smile. "I can tell you her problem," he said. "She is going to have a baby."

"That can't be," exclaimed Lilli. "She isn't even married."

"Being married has nothing to do with her condition.

She and Tom have been 'sleeping together' for several months. I can assure you, she is pregnant."

"What will she do? We will need to tell Tom and have the wedding for them immediately," Lilli asserted. "Her parents will be very upset with her. They are quite religious and won't approve of her having a child without a husband."

"I will leave that part up to you and Vickie. She will need to tell Tom and make the necessary arrangements with him. This is a job for the two women in my life," he explained.

Chapter 30

Vickie kept trying to explain to Tom the fact that she was going to have his baby. He was having no part of that fact. He flew into a rage accusing her of trying to entrap him into a marriage that he did not want. He had no intention of being encumbered with a wife and kid at his young age. Besides, he screamed at her, she wasn't his only 'woman'. He had many girlfriends on campus and none of them seemed to be going to have a baby. Vickie collapsed into a fit of uncontrollable weeping. She had no idea that he had other 'women'. She was so in love with him that she was convinced that he was 'true' to her. Although it seemed obvious to others that Tom as not loyal to anyone except himself, she had been oblivious to his outside behavior. She had dismissed his absences from her as just his way. Now she was forced to realize that he had never cared for her other than as a bed partner.

When Vickie finally got control of her emotions, she headed straight for Lilli to tell her the sad truth. Tom did not intend to marry her. She would need to have the baby all alone. Just saying those words made her shudder. How could she tell her mother that she had been promiscuous? She shivered in shame when she even thought of how she would present this fact to her mother. It would not be a pretty sight. Her parents were not rich and could barely afford life for themselves. It had been quite a sacrifice to send her to school; now she had spoiled all that be getting pregnant. Her career would end just before she was to graduate. She could no longer become a teacher; she would be a mother. When she related all this to Lilli, she fell into hysterics again and was crying uncontrollably until she nearly passed out from exhaustion.

Lilli hurried to find Grayson to help her console Vickie and to calm her. Lilli was concerned that Vickie was so frail that she might lose the baby, a fact that might make Tom happy, but would only complicate the situation for Vickie. Grayson met with the girls in their dorm room and began to try to sooth Vickie's ravaged feelings. He tried to explain to her that having a baby was a normal experience. Many young women had babies without husbands. He tried to assure her that her parents would understand after the initial shock wore off. Vickie didn't believe his story of how her parents might react. She knew that they would be very upset and would blame her completely for this misfortune. Her biggest concern was what she would do after she had the baby. Where would she go? Who would take care of her? How could she take care of herself? If she went back to Otwell, she would not be able to find a job and she would be at the mercy of her mother and dad for the rest of her life. And, she was convinced that no other man would ever want a 'soiled woman'. Grayson tried to reassure her that she was too distraught to think clearly. Many of the things that she was envisioning would not come to pass. Her parents would surely welcome her and their grandchild. And, someday she would find a suitable husband who would love her and take care of her and her child.

As the evening wore on, the three of them stayed in the room, trying to console Vickie. She finally fell asleep from sheer exhaustion. Grayson and Lilli slipped out of the room and went to the dining hall to find something to eat. They enjoyed the meal although their conversation was centered on Vickie and her dilemma. They had not ready answers.

Lilli agreed with Vickie's consensus of her parents. She was certain that they would not be very receptive in the beginning, but would eventually take care of Vickie and the child. Grayson felt such a responsibility for Vickie and stated that he should have told her more about Tom's behavioral patterns. He had never been certain how he should have approached the subject with her. Now it was too late.

The two of them gathered some food to take to the room for Vickie. When they returned she was still sleeping soundly. Lilli stored the food in a cabinet for her to eat another day, and covered Vickie with a blanket to keep her warm as she continued sleeping. She kissed Grayson goodnight and he left the two women in the room together. He left with a heavy heart. He still wasn't sure what his role in this dilemma should be but he felt a great deal of compassion for Vickie in her hour of need. He would have to think about what he could do to help her.

Chapter 31

Everyone on campus was preparing for graduation. Lilli would be getting her diploma and she would need to find a job. She really wanted to stay in Evansville. She had no intention of going back to Otwell for any reason. She wanted to develop a life in the city. There were several schools near the college where she could possibly get a job. She would have to apply through the Evansville School District and request that she get a placement in a school within walking distance, if possible. She did not have a car, so it was important to her that she find a job within near where she lived. As soon as graduation was over, she would seek out a good school where she could begin her career in teaching.

Grayson had decided that he would go on to medical school at Indiana University near Indianapolis. Lilli hated to see him make this decision. She wanted him to pursue his career in Evansville, but he was convinced that he wanted to become a doctor. He was still laboring over the dilemma that Vickie was in at this time. She was preparing to graduate and she could easily disguise her condition under her gown that she would wear for the graduation. She had not yet told her parents of her condition. She convinced Lilli that she wanted that 'sheepskin' before she told anyone. She also felt that she should tell Tom's parents hoping that they might make him support her and her baby. But, she had to get through the graduation ceremony first. She had really studied hard to bring up her grades to be able to graduate when she realized her condition.

Tom Howard was not going to graduate. His grades were abysmal and in fact, he probably would need to try to get into another school.

In fact, it seemed that he had simply disappeared from campus. No one seemed to know where he was. His father had gone to the college and inquired of his whereabouts. No one seemed to know where he might be. He contacted Lilli and Vickie but they had no knowledge of him. Vickie lied when she told them that she hadn't seen him since his jail experience. Lilli corroborated her story. Mr. Howard seemed distraught and left rather forlornly with the news that his son had simply disappeared from the campus.

The graduation ceremony was a lovely event. Lilli and Vickie and Grayson proudly walked in the procession across the stage to receive their diplomas. The speaker for the evening stated that the "World was Their Oyster". So many exciting things were happening in the world around them. The automobile industry was booming and soon cars would be everywhere. The telegraph industry was soon to be a major player in the commerce and medicine was making great strides in the preventative side of medicine as well as the treatment of diseases. The speaker referenced the fact that the

'Great War to End All Wars' had just ended. Young men could now seek careers for themselves and their families in modern commerce. The two girls listened with rapt attention although the speaker did not mention any careers for women, only men. However, Lilli knew what her career was and she was determined to become a good teacher. Grayson was enthralled with the speaker and felt buoyed by his reference to medical technology. When the evening was over, Grayson took the girls out for a soda at the local drug store. He spoke gloriously about his next step in his career and his plan to go on to the University to pursue his dream of becoming a doctor.

The girls went back to their room and began to discuss their next step. They would be moving out of the dorm by the weekend. Lilli would be looking for an apartment very early the next morning. Vickie would need to contact her parents for a ride back to Otwell. Both the girls crawled into their beds and knew that tomorrow would bring a new experience for both of them. Lilli had no idea how the new day would affect her.

Chapter 32

Lilli arose early in the morning and went to the lobby of the dormitory to find a newspaper. She was sipping coffee and perusing the ads in the paper looking for an apartment. She found a few listed in the near neighborhood. She finished her coffee, took her notepad and left the building heading down the street to the first place on her list.

Grayson arrived shortly after Lilli left the building. He went straight to her room thinking that she would be there. When he knocked on the door, Vickie came to the door. She was fully dressed and was packing her things. She was rehearsing her speech that she would be giving to her mother when she called them to come and get her. Grayson stepped inside the room and asked about Lilli.

"She was gone when I got up," Vickie said.

"Where did she go, do you know?"

"I think she went apartment hunting. That's what she told me last night before we went to bed."

"I have been thinking about a lot of things, Vickie," Grayson began. "I know you are in a terrible state of mind about your condition. I have given this a great deal of thought in the last few days, and I have decided that I want to marry you."

"You want to what?" Vickie screamed.

"I want to marry you. You haven't told anyone except Lilli and me about your condition, have you?"

"No, I wanted to tell Mr. Howard, but I felt that I should tell my mother first. I am still working on my speech that I will need to give to her. Why would you want to marry me? I am carrying another man's child."

Grayson walked closer to the woman who was his girlfriend's best friend and tried to answer her questions. "I can't tell you that I am in love with you, but I certainly respect you. I know that you are a kind and caring person. I am sure that you will be a good mother to your baby. And, I feel that you will be a good wife for me. I am going to be a doctor, so I will know how to take care of you and the baby. I am going away to Bloomington to school, so no one needs to be the wiser about the paternity of your baby. Will you say yes to my marriage proposal?"

Vickie sat down on the bed and held her head in her hands. The tears returned involuntarily. How could such a fine young man want to marry her? She had 'soiled' herself by believing in a man who had no morals about him. Now, one of the finest young men that she had ever met was offering her a lifetime of cover-up for her baby and herself. How could she refuse him? Was she afraid of her parents or was she just eager to solve her own problem? And, what would Lilli say? How could she marry the man who loved her best friend? Vickie looked up at Grayson through her tear flooded eyes and asked, "What will Lilli think if I marry her 'man'?"

"I have not discussed this with Lilli. I made the decision on my own during the night. Lilli will have to understand your circumstances and the solution that I am offering you. She will be upset but hopefully understanding."

Vickie rose to her feet and hugged the man who was going to become her husband as soon as possible. Grayson left the room, and Vickie continued packing her belongings. Grayson assured her that he would be back in the evening to load his car for their move to Bloomington. They would get a license when they got to the University, and be married by a preacher there. They would go through Otwell and advise her parents on their way out of town.

As Grayson was walking down the sidewalk on the way back to his room at his rooming house, he saw Lilli walking toward him as she was going back toward the dorm. She had found an apartment and she was heading home to pack her stuff to move in yet that very evening. He pulled his car over to the curb and she willingly got inside. "Let me take you to lunch, he said. I have some news for you." Lilli willingly got in his car and leaned back to relax. She began to babble about the nice apartment that she had found in a house on Bellemeade Avenue. It was a large room in the back of a widow's home. She would have a private entrance and cooking privileges. She was very happy with the location, and now all she had to do was to begin looking for a job through the Evansville School System at some of the schools near the house.

Grayson and Lilli settled in the restaurant on Lincoln Avenue. It was a homey place and the smell of fried chicken permeated the entire atmosphere. Lilli did not realize how hungry she was until she began to smell the fragrances of food cooking. The waitress came to their table and the two of them ordered a full meal and ice tea to drink. Lilli could hardly wait for the tea to arrive since she had worked up quite a thirst from walking.

When they finished their meal, the waitress tried to entice them with coconut pie for dessert. Lilli decided that she didn't need anything else, but Grayson was tempted and conceded that he would like a nice piece of pie. When he finished his dessert, he leaned back in his chair and mentioned that he had some news to tell her. She thought for a moment that it might be a proposal. But, she already had her apartment, and she wondered how she could refuse his offer.

Grayson began by telling her that she was his one true love. He had fallen in love with her quite some time ago, but that circumstances had now changed the order of things. He wanted her to know how he felt about her. And that his love for her had not changed, but the circumstances had changed.

"I have asked Vickie to marry me," he stated with downcast eyes.

"You what," asked Lilli unbelievingly.

"I have asked her to marry me in order to give the baby a name and a life without shame," he continued. "She is in such dire straits, and that skunk, Tom Howard, has abandoned her. I will be a doctor and can take care of her and the baby. I am not in love with her," he continued, "but I will be able to give the baby a name and a life of its own without the shame of being a bastard child. I had hoped that you would understand my position."

Lilli was so stunned by his admission and decision that she could hardly think clearly. She took only a split second to reply to his statement about her understanding his position. As she saw his position, it was one of abandonment of her after all the years that they had been together.

"I certainly do understand your position, Grayson, and I will tell you that I can not give you my blessing. You are my first and only true love and I can't remove that from my mind that quickly. However, what you are doing is noble and considerate to Vickie, albeit a slap in my face. Thank you for my lunch, and may I never see you again in this life or the hereafter," she said as she stood and stormed out the door, tears streaming down her cheeks as she tried to hurry back to her new apartment. Grayson was behind her, wanting to discuss this more but she wanted no part of his story. "I will stay with her until the child is raised and then I will come back to you," he shouted as she walked down the sidewalk.

"No you won't, Grayson, I don't want a 'second-hand' husband. I will find my own," Lilli said, and she never looked back. She hurried to her new apartment and asked the landlady if she could spend the night there and move in the next day. Her landlady, a woman named Mabel Copley, agreed to allow her to stay and readily noticed that Lilli was distraught. The two of them sat down at the table and Lilli gave her the whole story. The bond that the two women forged that evening would never be broken.

Chapter 33

Morning came much sooner than Lilli had wanted. She had slept very little during the night. Her scene with Grayson that had taken place the afternoon before, was still running through her mind. Grayson was actually going to marry Vickie and leave her high and dry. They had been together almost two years and now he was going to forsake her. His marriage to Vickie was a noble gesture, and he was right when he said that it would provide her baby a father and a life that was without shame. And, he had admitted to her that he was not in love with Vickie but that he would make her a good husband, and she would be a good mother to the baby. Lilli could not bury her resentment.

She still had not seen Vickie since her lunch date with Grayson. She was sure that she had packed up and moved to Bloomington with him leaving the apartment empty. Lilli did not want to run into her when she went to get her own things from the apartment so she had asked Mabel if she could stay with her for a week or so making sure that Vickie and Grayson were gone. She had only the clothes that she was wearing, but it was a weekend, and she could exist in her current togs until she was sure that the 'newlyweds' were gone. She had no intention of running into either of them, ever again. She knew that she could 'double-cross' Vickie by telling the truth of her marriage to Grayson all around Otwell, but that was not the right thing for her to do. Deep inside, she felt a great deal of compassion for both of them because of the decisions that they had made; however, it still hurt to think that she had been abandoned by Grayson.

Lilli chose to get out of bed, dress in her same clothes, and wander down past his apartment house to see if Grayson's car was missing. She knew that she couldn't hide from them forever. Surely Vickie would want to say goodbye and perhaps apologize for what she was doing. And, Lilli would need to respond. She couldn't hate her. She had done nothing wrong to Lilli, and yet, she couldn't hate Grayson either. What he was doing was a noble deed. So, she decided that she would brace up her backbone and walk over to her apartment and face them if they were still there. She began to think about what she might say to them. If Vickie asked her to forgive her, she would be considerate and do so. If Grayson tried to apologize to her again, she would just dismiss him by saying that he had already said all that he needed to say to her by way of an explanation. She had her speech all made up in her mind. She knew how to handle this situation. She considered herself a 'big girl, and a well adjusted adult'. She would cry on her own time.

The morning air was a bit brisk, but it was refreshing as she walked toward her old dorm room. She had her speech all prepared and was ready to confront the two of them. When she reached his apartment house, she saw that Grayson's car was missing. She turned left and headed to her dormitory to retrieve her possessions so she could move into her new apartment. When she reached the apartment, she saw that Vickie was also gone. Her clothes and the few furniture items that she had were gone. Lilli assumed that the two of them had hurried out of town and gone on to Bloomington. When she began to gather her possessions together, she spied on the dresser an envelope with her name on it. She recognized Vickie's handwriting. Lilli picked it up and stuffed it into the box with her underwear and decided to read it later. She needed to get her things out of the dorm room and hurry back to her new apartment before she broke down again. Mabel would understand, she thought, and would help her recover from this trauma in her life.

Lillie packed her stuff in boxes and began the trek back to the house on Bellemeade where she would be living. It took three trips to get everything moved. She had forgotten how much stuff she really owned, and should have been better at tossing a lot of it, but right now, she wasn't in the mood to throw out stuff. She would try to sort it all out when she was safely in her own room. She wasn't sure that she was hurrying to get out and back to her room, or was she afraid that she would encounter the two of them. Regardless of her motive, she was busy and didn't have time to think about her dilemma.

It was early evening before she had managed to get everything unpacked. As she suspected, she had a large box of 'stuff' to discard but at least she had spent her time wisely by not allowing her mind to fester with resentment.

Lilli curled up in her big overstuffed chair and pulled out the envelope that was addressed to her. She held it close to her breast for a few moments before opening it.

Dear Lilli:

I know that you are probably very upset with me and especially with Grayson. Please try to understand that I had no idea that he would propose to me. He has admitted that he is not in love with me, but is doing this to give my baby a life of its own. As you would know, a 'bastard' baby in Otwell would not only be an outcast on his own, but would brand his mother as a 'fallen woman,' marking her for life. With that in mind, please understand that Grayson has not only saved my reputation, but the life of my child if forced to live in such a small town.

I know that I can depend on your secrecy for me and my family. I have loved you as a sister all the time that we have been together, and I hope that we will meet again and be friends for the rest of our lives.

Please forgive me for hurting you and keep me in your prayers just like we once did at the Otwell Baptist Church.

Love, Vickie

Chapter 34

Lillie folded the letter and placed it against her breast as the tears gently rolled down her cheeks. She remembered the days in the Otwell Baptist Church, but she had not been there in many years. Yes, she remembered the two girls would pray together at the altar and confess their momentary sins. They sang in the church choir which was comprised of so few kids that the choir loft seemed empty. They participated in the activities at the church on weekends that were offered for the young people of the community. Yes, Lilli could remember them. Maybe she needed to pray about them now. Maybe if she prayed about this situation, she would find peace within herself and not be so broken by her loss of her one true love. She leaned back in her chair and began to phrase in her mind, the prayer to help her understand her position in this matter. And, she prayed that she could forgive both of them, since what they were doing was not wrong, only hurtful to her.

After a long while, Lilli decided to knock on Mabel's door and see if she would join her in a pot of tea. She would talk with her and then she vowed to get on with her life, without Grayson and without Vickie.

Chapter 35

In a few short days, Lilli was offered a teaching job at one of the schools near her apartment. The Hanover School was within walking distance of the house where she lived. She would be teaching the third grade. She had met the Superintendent of the School system and explained where she lived and hoped that there would be an opening for her there. The Superintendent sent her to the principal of Hanover School. The Principal mentioned that he needed a teacher for the third grade and one for the sixth grade, but he felt she would do better with the younger students because it was her first teaching assignment. He mentioned that some of the sixth grade boys would be bigger than she was and that they might present a problem for her to discipline them if they misbehaved. Lillie agreed that the little ones would be better for her first experience.

The principal mentioned that school would not start until September and that there would be no work for her until then. She assured him that she would find work somewhere for the remaining summer months. She was to be paid $75.00 per month during the nine months that school was in session. Lilli signed the necessary papers and turned to leave the school building. The principal asked if she were walking or had a car. She stated that she was walking but that she lived only a few blocks away. He offered to drive her home, but she assured him that she needed the walk to think about her next move.

Lilli went down the steps with a renewed spirit and vigor. Her job would help her move her thought about Grayson to the back of her mind for the time being. She had a job for the school year. Now, she only needed to find one for the rest of the summer.

She hurried home to share with Mabel her new found success. And, she knew that it was lunch time and she was sure that Mabel would have something ready for her when she arrived.

Chapter 36

Summer was nearly over; Lilli had worked the little time left of the summer at a little café near her apartment. She had begun her job as a dishwasher, but soon worked her way up to taking lunch orders. She had been able to save most of her money that she made in tips so that she could purchase a few new sweaters and skirts for the coming school days. She also needed a new winter coat since she would be walking to school during the cold weather. She studied her shoe collection and decided that she would also need new shoes from her first school paycheck. Styles were beginning to change again, and she didn't want to look like 'last years old clothes'. Lillie liked to be stylish and she frequently studied the papers and magazines to see what the latest fashions were going to be for the coming year.

Mabel had taken her shopping a few times and the two women enjoyed each others' company. Mabel had shared with her the story of her own life the last few years. Mabel related how her husband had been killed loading a barge on the river, leaving her with one son to raise. Together the two of them had purchased and paid for the house where she lived, so she realized she had been well taken care of when he died. And the boy, who had been nine years old when his father was killed, became her helper around the house. She depended on her son for all the handy work that needed to be done.

But, when the flu ravaged the Evansville area, her son had become quite ill and died overnight, leaving Mabel all alone in the home that she and her husband had owned together. When Lilli heard her tell the story, she was so ashamed that she had burdened the woman with her 'pity party' over Vickie and Grayson that she could hardly express herself.

"I am so very sorry, Mabel," she began. Your life has been so much harder than mine. I am embarrassed that I burdened you with my tale of woe."

"Oh, no, Mabel replied, I could relate to your broken heart. You see, mine was broken twice, so I understood how you must have felt. I am glad that we have each other and that we can now go on with our lives together."

The two women stopped at a local soda shop and had a nice chocolate soda and laughed about the happenings in the world at the time.

Chapter 37

Summer was finally over and school was ready to begin. Mabel had been the 'fashion expert' each time that Lilli would complete an outfit for school. She would model the clothing for Mabel to see if it fit properly or if the color was good. Lilli wanted her wardrobe to be fashionable, yet in good taste for her new job.

In the evenings when she returned to her room, she often thought of Grayson and Vickie. She was determined to push them out of her mind; however, it was not an easy task. She wondered how they were doing and if they were having a happy life together. She tried to tell herself that she would find someone else in her life who could make her happy and that she should forget these two and what they had done to her. Often, as she drifted off to sleep, she would allow her mind to question what she had done wrong in her love affair with Grayson. Maybe she had been too 'easy' in giving herself to him. Maybe she should have kept herself from him until they were married as she had been taught to do. And, then there was the alcohol; maybe she had been influenced by it. She didn't have the answer to any of her questions.

Chapter 38

Labor Day was over and the first day of school began the day after the holiday. Lilli donned one of her new outfits and was ready to meet her students. The weather was nice and she left early enough to walk at a leisurely pace to school. She had visited the school the week before and prepared her room for the class. She had posters on the wall, and the alphabet written in script as well as lower case on the black board. She would have a room full of 1st and 2nd graders, so the principal had told her and she was more than anxious to begin her career path. When she arrived at school, the secretary to the principal told her that she had a letter in the school office. Lilli was certain that Mother had written to her in response to one that she had written home. She had informed Mother that she had an apartment and a new job. Then, she wondered why Mother would write to her at the school, since she had her home address.

She hurriedly took the letter and looked at the return address. That space was blank on the envelope, but she noticed that the postmark was Bloomington, Indiana. She stuck the letter down in her purse and went on to her classroom. If she chose to read the letter at all, she would do it in the evening.

Her class was full and boisterous. They were typically 1st and 2nd graders who had played outside all summer and now could not conceive of settling down into a classroom. Lilli finally got their attention and promised them that she would read a story to them once they had their seat assignment completed. She placed the 1st graders on her right and the 2nd graders on her left. She decided against arranging them alphabetically since many of them had the same last names. She casually glanced over all the children and arbitrarily seated them in rows. In the 2nd grade she had some boys who had obviously not been to many school classes because she judged them to be about 12 years old. They were really too big for the seats, but she wasn't sure that she could get bigger desks for them. She made a note and decided that she would discuss it with the principal after school. She didn't try to memorize the names of the children on the first day, but she knew that soon she would need to be able to call each of them by name.

When school was finally over, she started her leisurely walk home. She found the walk refreshing since she had been so occupied with classroom activities during the day. She was concerned with how to seat each student as well as how she could teach both grades in the same room. She wanted each student to get the best education that she could give them, but just how she could accomplish that remained to be seen by such a new experience. But she loved the challenge and she was buoyed on to her apartment with the thoughts of how she could accomplish her goals.

Reaching her house, she went up on the porch and

seemed to drop into the porch swing. Mabel had seen her coming down the street and met her on the porch with a cold glass of iced tea for each of them and a couple of fresh baked peanut butter cookies for them to share. Lilli began to ramble on and on about the events of the day and the various children whom she had encountered. She mentioned the bigger boys and how they hardly fit in the seats. Mabel listened to her tell the stories of the day. Suddenly, Lilli remembered the letter in her pocket. She pulled it from its secure hiding place and pushed it across the small table for Mabel to look at. "It hasn't been opened," Mabel mused.

"No, I haven't opened it. I am not sure if I want to open it. What could it possibly say that I haven't heard before? More apologies? More explanations about why it happened the way that it did? I don't need to hear any more of those stories, Mabel. I have heard them all. I think I shall just keep it for a while and see if I ever need to read it in the future.

I think that I have time for a little nap before dinner," Lilli said as she gathered her books together and slowly went to her room. Once inside her room, she opened a small box that once had held some jewelry of hers, and she placed the letter inside the box. Glancing around the room, she thought she needed a good place to keep the box that would not be of any interest to anyone else. She finally decided to place the box on the top shelf of her closet out of eyesight or easy reach of anyone. After she had safely deposited the box in its resting place, she slipped off her shoes and quickly laid across the bed for a short nap. When she awoke, Mabel was announcing that dinner was awaiting her arrival. She had slept for more than an hour.

Chapter 39

The school year was progressing nicely. Lilli had grown to love her students. Some of them were quite anxious to learn to read and to write but some of them had no interest in learning much. She determined that the slower students might be too young to be in school and perhaps their mother's had sent them to school to get some rest at home. The bigger boys were more of a problem than the slow learning children. They didn't want to be in school at all, but were attending because otherwise they would be working in the farm fields at home. Lilli found that the biggest challenge that she had was to keep the bigger boys busy and to help them learn at a higher level than the other 2nd graders.

Almost everyday, there was another letter from Bloomington waiting for her in her box in the office. She wondered if the other teachers were aware of the secret that was transpiring in the office concerning her. She never mentioned any of her past life to anyone except Mabel. If the other teachers wondered what was going on, they never mentioned it to her.

Each day she took the letter home and placed it in the box on the top shelf, unopened. Although she was curious about what the letters said, but she was certain that it was more of the same. The handwriting varied on the letters and she knew that some of them were from Vickie and some were from Grayson. However, she did not intend to open them, at least for now.

Chapter 40

Winter was beginning to arrive in Evansville. It was becoming harder and harder for Lilli to walk to school. The city buses were running in some areas, but it was farther to a bus stop than it was for her to walk to school. On some really rainy days, Mabel had taken her to school, but Lilli didn't like to impose on her. She began to question Mabel about buying a car of her own. She had saved most of her money that she had been making during the fall. When she had enough money, she would like to buy a car of her own.

Mabel had a friend who knew more about cars than she did, and she began to question him about helping Lilli find a car of her own.

After school one afternoon, Mabel's friend was waiting for Lilli at the school with a car for her to consider. He assured her that he would be glad to teach her how to drive the vehicle before the winter snows began to fall. Lilli was favorably impressed with the salesman and the car. He told her that the car would cost her $290.00 if she wanted to buy it, and that he would be available to help her learn to drive it as well as help her take care of it until she could learn all the details of car ownership. Lilli responded to the sales pitch and the trial ride in the car. She told him that she would consider his offer, but that she needed to discuss it with Mabel and to check her finances. He assured her that he completely understood and would check with her in a few days. Then, he finally introduced himself as Wesley Theron. Lilli shook his hand and slowly got out of the car and climbed the steps to her house. She needed to think over the prospect of owning a car and she needed to check her cache' of money. Did she have enough to buy a car and if so, did she choose to spend it that way?

Mabel was waiting at the kitchen table with a cup of hot tea and a plate of cookies. She stated that all decisions are made over tea and cookies. Lilli didn't argue with her about that point.

When school was over the very next day, Lilli noticed that there was a car waiting at the end of the walk by the school. As she neared the car, she realized that Wesley was waiting for her in the car. She opened the door to climb in the passenger's side, but he had jumped out of the driver's side and motioned for her to come to that side of the car. He courteously showed her how to get in the car, and how to operate the manual gears. He showed her what she needed to do to start the engine, and then he slowly climbed into the other side of the car. She sat in the driver's seat for a long moment, realizing that she had not bought this car yet, but Wesley was teaching her how to drive it. She laughed at his salesmanship. She surmised that he thought if she knew how to drive it, it would be easy to sell it to her. And, he was probably right. She and Mabel had discussed the situation over their tea and cookies the evening before, and Lilli had decided to spend her savings on the car. She wanted to take a trip back to Otwell to see Mother and Dad before the weather turned too cold or before the snow began to fall. Would she know how to drive the car that far by then? She would just have to wait and see.

Lilli and Wesley went to the dealership where the car was being sold. Wesley asked her if she felt comfortable purchasing the car. Lilli stalled in her response, and he chimed in that the driving instructions came with the purchase. He smiled at Lilli when he made the statement and she quickly caught his intentions. There was nothing wrong with Wesley. She thought him to be a kind and considerate man but she was still harboring a broken heart from what Grayson had done to her. She wasn't sure that she was interested in another man at this time. Before she could make a statement, Wesley pushed the sales ticket across the table for her to sign. Then, he placed his hand over hers and, glancing into her eyes, he said, "If you want to talk this over, I would like to treat you to dinner tonight."

Lilli didn't know how to answer, but she hadn't had a date in a long time. She would need to tell Mabel that she wouldn't be home for dinner if she accepted his offer. "I couldn't go tonight, because I haven't informed Mabel that I won't be home for dinner," Lilli replied.

"That won't be necessary; I took the liberty of inviting her to join us since I was sure that your decision needs to have her blessing."

Lilli could hardly say no to such a proposition. If Wesley had invited Mabel to join them, then she did not have a good excuse. "I am not sure that I am dressed appropriately for dinner," she said.

"You look fine, Lilli, and I will take us all to a local restaurant that isn't a fancy dress-up place."

Wesley helped Lilli into the passenger's seat, and went to the driver's side. He proceeded to drive over to pick up Mabel and the threesome went to a local restaurant to have a meal.

While the three of them enjoyed an evening meal, the conversation turned to Lilli's job at the school. Mabel mentioned that she had just graduated from Evansville College and had been able to get a job teaching almost immediately. Wesley turned to Lilli and asked her where she had lived before she came to Mabel's house. "I lived on campus," she said. There was a lull in the conversation. Lilli knew that he wanted to know where her home was, but she wasn't ready to reveal anything to him. She still felt a little apprehensive about divulging her background. She knew there was a mystery there, and until she could figure it all out, she wasn't going to talk about it.

Chapter 41

Lilli did purchase the car from Wesley. She had practiced driving the car all around Evansville. Mabel and Lilli took frequent trips to the Main street to shop on Saturday afternoons. It was not long before Lilli felt that she could drive her car anywhere.

Wesley had been true to his word. He helped her understand that she needed to have the oil in the motor changed frequently and what she should do if she had a flat tire. In addition to giving her accurate instructions on how to own a car, Wesley frequently took her and Mabel to dinner at local restaurants. Lilli was certain that he was developing strong feelings for her and she knew that she should be responding appropriately, but, she just didn't seem to be falling in love. She discussed her inability to respond with Mabel who simply told her that it takes time to develop a love life.

School was about to be out for the summer, and Lilli needed to find another summer job. One afternoon when she returned home from school, Mabel told her that the man who owned the restaurant where she had worked during the past summer before had stopped by and talked with her about Lilli working again for the coming season. It would be an opportunity for Lilli to put the money that she had spent for the car back into her savings account and have more money for new clothes before school started again. It seemed like a good idea to Lilli and she hurried down to the café to inform the owner that she would be happy to work again for the summer.

Chapter 42

Lilli stayed with Mabel for the next few years. She loved her apartment and the camaraderie that she had with her landlady. It seemed that the two were meant to be together. Wesley continued to stop by and visit with Lilli and occasionally took her to dinner. Mabel often cooked for the three of them, making sure that Wesley was informed of a good home cooked meal and she made sure that he was welcome. It was obvious to Mabel and Lilli that Wesley wanted to be considered a 'paramour' of Lilli but she still maintained her distance.

Her letters continued to arrive from Bloomington. She had not opened a single one. It became necessary for her to get a bigger box to hold them, but she still continued to leave them unopened. She often wondered how long it would take her to forget Grayson, but it didn't seem to be happening now. And, each time she received a letter, it was like opening the old wound again.

Summer was just around the corner. Lilli had been teaching at the school for five years. She had not been home to see Mother and Dad since she had graduated from college. She was pondering whether or not she should take her summer job this year. Perhaps she should travel back to Otwell and visit with friends and family. She felt quite comfortable driving her car and if she started early in the morning, she could make the trip before the afternoon was over.

When the school year ended, she announced to Mabel that she would be making a trip to Otwell this summer. Mabel's first question was concerning Wesley. Would he be going with her? Lilli made no hesitation when she answered a resounding "no". She was going alone. She wanted to visit with family and friends on her own time.

Early one June morning, Lilli loaded her clothes in her car and left for the trip to Otwell. It was not an easy trip, but the weather was beautiful and scenery was lovely. The dogwood trees seem to be beckoning to her to visit her childhood home. She had always loved the flowers and trees that bloomed in the spring. She also knew that Mother would have early June peas and new potatoes to cook. Lilli's mouth began to water just thinking about the early vegetables that Mother would prepare for her while she was visiting in her home town. As she traveled along the gravel and dirt roads, she was reminded of a lot of the things she had pushed out of her mind over the years. When she crossed over the bridges that spanned a creek or river, she remembered playing in the waters and looking for frogs. She was also reminded of her fear of snakes that had kept her from wandering through the woods in the heat of the summer. In the spring, she often had gone hunting for mushrooms in the woods. She was quite adept at finding the big morels but she was sure that the season for mushrooms was over for the year.

As she traveled along, she realized that she was hungry. Mabel had packed her a lunch, and as she went through the town of Oakland City, she paused in the park long enough to eat the sandwich. She realized that she had not taken the time to do many leisurely activities in the past 10 years. Today was to be the beginning of her taking time for the simple things in her life. She finished her lunch and headed back up the road toward Otwell.

Lilli finally saw a few of the landmarks that she could remember from her childhood. It had been many years since she had been back here. She saw the little white Baptist church where she had been a member for many years. She also remembered the cemetery next to the church where she had played 'hide and seek' with her friends as they romped through the tombstones. She remembered the old hymns that she had sung from the choir as a child. She had often wanted to wander through the cemetery to read the gravestones but she had never taken the time to do that. "This trip, I will do that," she said to herself. "And, I will ride a horse again, and gather eggs from the barn, and milk the old cow like I did so many years ago."

As the car chugged down the roads Lilli was amazed at how the small towns that she had known as a young girl had grown to have more than just a general store in them. Some of them had town halls, libraries, doctor's offices, and saloons. It was hard for her to comprehend how much progress had taken place in the last ten years.

But she was a grown woman now, with a career and a car. She was 28 years old and still single. When that thought came to her mind, she did not think of Wesley, but of Grayson. She wondered how old she would be before he would be out of her thoughts. And, would it be fair to Wesley if she married him while Grayson was still in her heart?

Soon she was driving up the familiar road in the middle of Otwell. She by-passed her family's driveway and circled through town. She was completely amazed at what she saw. There was a hardware store, a feed store, a 10cent store, a dentist's office, a jewelry store, a restaurant, and a saloon on the main street that seemed to be teeming with people where it had once quite barren. On the other side of the street were even more shops. It seemed to be a thriving town which was a far cry from what she had known in her youth.

She circled the block in her car and saw a number of men standing near the corner. They seemed to be watching her every move. She was a stranger in their town, but even more surprising was that she was a woman driving a car. Most women did not drive a car in 1928. Lilli was different.

She drove up into the yard of the house where she had spent her entire life until she was 18 years old. It looked much the same. Under the front porch was an old dog, just like always. He seemed to be enjoying the summer weather, and he barely opened his eyes to greet her. The maple trees in the front yard were completely leafed out and offered shade for the porch that held a familiar swing and two old rockers. The front door was open and the screen was keeping the insects at bay. Lilli stepped up onto the porch but before she could knock, Mother was opening the screen. The words were forming on her lips to ask this stranger what she wanted, when she realized it was Lilli. She yelled to her husband that it was Lilli at the door. The two of them came out onto the porch and began to hug her. Mother started to cry, now that her daughter was home.

"Who brought you home?"

"No one, Mother."

"Whose car is that?"

"It is my car, Dad. I bought it a few years ago to drive back and forth to school."

"No woman owns a car, Lilli. What were you thinking?" he responded.

"Why wouldn't I own a car?"

"It just isn't lady-like; you need a husband," Dad retorted.

"I'm sorry to disappoint you, Dad, but I don't have a husband, and I can not understand why I should walk to school in the winter if I can afford a car."

"Well, women shouldn't work anyway; they should be wives and mothers."

Lilli was hurt to see that she was welcomed by such harsh words. When Dad had such an outburst on his first meeting with her in several years, she wondered why she felt compelled to visit Otwell.

She turned to Mother and began to try to talk to her about what was going on in the community. She soon discovered that Mother was quiet and could hardly talk to her because of the interruptions of Dad.

As the afternoon wore on, the three people visited and walked around the yard. Lilli felt a little uncomfortable around them. She realized that Mabel had moved her consciousness into the modern world around her and that Mother and Dad still lived in earlier times.

Their evening meal was tasty and the apple pie that Mother had baked was a delight. Lilli had forgotten how good Mother's apple pies were, and that she would just have that for breakfast, too. Dad then spoke up and stated that people did not eat pie for breakfast; she would need to eat what everyone else ate, sausage, biscuits, gravy, and eggs. Just another demand, thought Lilli.

Chapter 43

When the sun came streaming through her bedroom window, Lilli awoke to the smell wafting through her bedroom door that was ajar, of breakfast cooking in the kitchen. She hurriedly dressed and went to the kitchen to help. She realized that Mother was still cooking on the same old iron monster of a stove in the kitchen. She wondered why she didn't have a more modern stove like a Kerosene one. Although it was still early June, it was quite hot in the kitchen because of the coal stove that had been fired-up to make the oven hot enough to bake biscuits.

Suddenly Lilli realized that her family did not have indoor plumbing and that the old out-house was still in use. She cringed at the thought that she would need to visit it before she did anything to help Mother. Slowly she understood how she had progressed away from 'country' living by simply going to college in a nearby city. Although she didn't think she could help them in any way, it was not because she didn't want to help, but because Dad would not allow her help. He even seemed to resent her success.

When the breakfast dishes were cleared and the kitchen cleaned, Lilli went outside with her mother. They walked around the yard and talked lightly about all the flowers, the dogs, and the farm animals. She asked Lilli how she was doing and what her job was at the school. She carefully avoided mentioning any conflict with Dad, but Lilli could see that there were definite problems between them. She was shocked at how much of a dictator Dad really was. When she watched the two of them together, she was alarmed at how little respect he had for his wife. Somehow she hadn't noticed these things when she was young but now, in adulthood, it was obvious to her.

The two women sat in the porch swing that was gently swaying back and forth as they talked about the news of the day and the news of the past. Mother began to tell Lilli of how her father had progressed to his state of mind. "He has always been the one in control but lately he has also become quite belligerent. He has 'spells' of not remembering ordinary things like knowing when he milked the cows last. I have tried to be patient with him, but he seems to be getting worse in his behavior. Sometimes, I am almost afraid of him when I do something that he doesn't like."

"Oh, Mother, I am so sorry that you have to endure this from him. Do you think he is just getting old? Maybe he just has bad days."

"No, Lilli, he is really forgetful, and sometimes I have to remind him that it is time to gather the eggs or milk the cows. And, sometimes I have to remind him what my name is. He seems to forget everything. I wonder what I will ever do if he tries to hurt me."

"Do you think he would hurt you?"

"Once, when I got up in the night to go out to the outhouse, after I returned, he was waiting at the door with a club." I had to run around the house to get away from him because he thought I was a burglar."

Lilli pondered the stories that her mother was telling her. She had read about people who lost their minds as they aged, but she hadn't even considered that it would happen in her family.

The two women continued to visit on the porch until Dad came out to demand that Mother fix his breakfast. "We ate breakfast hours ago, Dad."

"I don't care what you say, I want my breakfast now. And you can go back to wherever you came from, because I don't even know you," he screamed.

Lilli simply walked away from the confrontation and decided to take a walk down the road. She wasn't sure what her dad meant when he stated that he 'didn't even know her'. Surely he did. He had raised her. She was hardly able to handle all this commotion. She only wanted to enjoy a trip home.

She remembered her vow to visit the church cemetery. She wanted to visit the church and pray for Mother and Dad. She would pray for patience for Mother to deal with her Dad. As she ventured down the road to the church, she noticed the spring flowers were all poking their heads through the underbrush. She stopped to pick a few violets just to hold them in her hand and smell them.

When she reached the church, she noted a buggy in the yard. She went to the door and found it open. She entered the sanctuary and looked around. The sight of the choir area brought tears to her eyes. She had not been in the choir in years. She walked up the two steps and sat in the pew for the choir. She was reminiscing about the times when she and Vickie had sung together in the old church. As she was thinking about 'old times', she heard a voice behind her asking if he could help her. She turned and saw a distinguished gentleman coming up beside her.

"Oh, no, I was just visiting the church of my youth," she replied. "I was a member here as a child and often sang in this choir with my friend, Vickie. I have not been back to Otwell in several years, and I just wanted to renew my 'spirit' by visiting here again."

"I am so glad you came in today," the man stated. "I am the pastor here and my name is Rev. Arnold. Do you plan to return to Otwell to live, miss?"

"No, I live in Evansville where I teach school. I am her visiting Mother and Dad, Mary Jane and Andrew Horton. I will be returning to Evansville tomorrow or the next day. I only wanted to visit the church, and I would also like to wander through the cemetery if I may. I played there as a child and the gravestones have long held a fascination for me."

"Allow me to accompany you through the cemetery. It is the time of year that the snakes are awakening from their sleep and you don't want to startle one of them into striking."

Lilli and Rev. Arnold left the church and walked through the path to the cemetery. It seemed strange to Lilli that so many of the people that she once knew were now buried in the cemetery. Her school teacher from the early part of the century was buried under a large oak tree. The lady who had given her a few piano lessons was also buried nearby. As the two of them walked through the graves, it seemed uncanny that Lilli had forgotten so many of the people from the church. She silently punished herself that she had not returned before now.

As the pair turned to walk back to the church, Lilli noticed that there was a small headstone that held the name of "Elayne". She stopped. It was an unusual spelling of the name and she wondered if that was where Mother got her name. Maybe she knew this woman. Then she saw the date on the headstone. It was January 1, 1900. The woman's name was Lula Elayne Jackson. How strange. The woman died on her birthday and her name was very near hers. Cold chills ran down her spine. She instantly knew that there was a secret to this name and date. Lilli had never been told the story of her birth. When she asked why her name was Jackson and Mother's name was Horton, she was always told that she was named after a relative.

Lilli turned to the preacher and stated that she needed to hurry home and help with the next meal. She could hardly contain her anxiety. Did the preacher know the story? Did he know that she had just discovered a part of her history? Who or where was her father? Would Mother tell her the truth? She wanted to run all the way home. She left the preacher standing in the graveyard somewhat mystified as to why she needed to leave so hastily.

When she entered the back door, she could smell ham cooking for the evening meal. She decided that she would control her enthusiasm and questions until after the evening meal. She wasn't sure if she wanted to confront the two of them or should she just wait and talk to Mother when they were alone.

She quickly helped Mother prepare a meal for the three of them. Then she almost single handedly cleaned the kitchen while Mother went to help Dad with the milking and gathering the eggs. All the time that she was washing dishes, she was planning how she would approach the subject with the two people in this house.

When the meal was over, the kitchen cleaned and all the chores were finished, Lilli suggested that they gather around the table for an evening of conversation. Dad was adamant about not joining the women, so Lilli agreed that she would just talk with Mother.

"I wandered through the cemetery today, Mother." She saw Mother arch her back as if she knew what was coming next. "I saw a gravestone with the name of Lula Elayne Jackson on it who died on the day I was born." Can you tell me if that is a coincidence or is there a story behind it?

Mother bowed her head and Lilli watched as the tears fell onto the checkered table cloth. "No, Lilli, it isn't a coincidence. She was your birth mother. She died within hours of your birth."

"Who is my father? Where is he? Does he know where I am?"

Mother wiped her eyes with the dish towel and began to tell the story of a troubled young man who did not have any idea how to raise a child. He needed to tend his farm and try to care for a baby. He had never had siblings so he had no experience in raising a child. He hardly knew how to start such a life. "He was a wonderful, hard working, honest man, Lilli. You should be proud to be his daughter."

As Mother was telling the story of her birth father, Dad, who had been listening in the other room, came bursting into the kitchen.

"He was a scoundrel to give away his daughter. I hope I never see him again," Dad screamed.

"But, Dad, Mother interjected, he gave you his farm and all his livestock plus his wonderful daughter whom you have loved as your own."

"I don't care; a child is not a pup that can be passed around; he is a scoundrel" he bellowed as he stormed out the back door.

Lilli was shocked to see such an outburst out of her dad. She was certainly shocked to hear the story of the gift of the farm and livestock.

"Did he really give you his farm and animals?"

"Yes, Lilli, he gave us everything he had in this world, including you. He came in our front door carrying a big brass key to the front door of his house, saying that he had nothing to offer us except his possessions." With this statement, Mother began to sob uncontrollably.

"I knew the day would come when I would need to explain it all to you, but I didn't know that Dad had held this anger all these years. Your biological mother was very young and sick. Your father did the only thing he knew to do and I have thanked God for his generosity for your entire life. I would have no child if he had not given us his."

"But where is he now, Mother? I didn't see but one headstone. Does he live nearby? Can I go see him?"

"I am sorry to say that I do not know where he is. He brought you to us when you were just a few hours old, and then he rode away toward the west. We have never seen him again."

"Oh, Mother, he must be so tortured by his decision to leave me, if he is as honorable as you say. How can I find him?"

"Lilli, I have no idea where you might start looking. I only know that he rode his horse down the road to the West."

Lilli hugged Mother, whispering in her ear that she loved her as a mother as she slowly carried her empty coffee cup to the sink. She had too much on her mind to talk any more. Her trip to Otwell had brought more news that she had expected, and it also brought a big mystery for her to try and solve. How could she find George Jackson, her biological father?

Chapter 44

Lilli tried to sleep but it seemed to elude her. She could not stop thinking about her real mother who must have suffered a lot giving birth to her. And, then she wondered where she should start looking for George Jackson. There were a lot of small towns between Otwell and Evansville. He could be anywhere. Maybe he had changed his name. She turned and tossed in the bed that she had slept in most of her young life. Tonight it didn't seem to give her the rest that she craved.

As she continued trying to find a way to fall asleep, she heard a commotion in the next room. She could hear Mother trying to stop her dad from shouting. He seemed completely out of control. She wondered if she should try to help. She heard the back door slam, and she knew that he had gone outside. Then the house grew quiet. No doubt, Mother had endured many of these nights. Lilli knew that Dad was not well and she wondered what would happen to him when Mother could not control him any longer. As the sun began streaming through the window, she realized she had been awake all night. She turned over and faced the wall and began counting the spots on the wallpaper just as she had done as a child, before finally drifting off to sleep.

Lilli finally made it to the breakfast table and noticed that Dad was at the table drinking coffee. He seemed docile and calm as he was eating his meal. She looked at Mother and winked. The two women seemed to understand each other.

Lilli ate her meal and stated that she would leave and return to Evansville as soon as the kitchen had been cleaned. She saw the tears well up in Mother's eyes, but she was stoic and continued with her plan. She had many things to think about and a long trip ahead of her.

She loaded her bags in the car and went to the driver's seat. Dad was there watching her as she started the engine. He looked perplexed to think a woman could drive that machine. She hugged Mother and quietly told her that she would stay in touch. She felt ashamed that she was leaving the problems regarding her father behind for Mother to contend with but she had her own brand of traumas to deal with as she returned to her life in Evansville.

During the trip across the many country roads that seemed to stretch on and on as she traveled back toward Mabel and her apartment, Lilli continued to try and sort out the information that she had about her birth parents. She knew that her real mother had died in childbirth at the age of 16. She also knew that the farm would probably be hers someday, but she really didn't think she wanted it. She was certain that she would never return to Otwell to live. And, now, the news of her birth which she had been told would eat at her until she could find her real father.

Lilli arrived at her apartment just after the sun had

slid down behind the horizon. She was welcomed by Mabel who had no idea when she was going to return, but she managed to put together a great meal for her to enjoy. As the two women sat at the table drinking tea, Lilli mentioned that she had a strange story to tell her.

Chapter 45

The two women, who had forged such a friendship, finished cleaning the kitchen after enjoying their fine evening meal. Their conversations over the dishpan were about events that had happened in Evansville while Lilli was in Otwell. Soon, Mabel could contain her curiosity no longer and she suggested that they move to the parlor in order for Lilli to speak of her new adventure.

Lilli went into great detail about the discovery of Father's belligerent temper and how he was treating Mother. She wondered if Mother was really in danger. Mabel related that she had known a few people who became violent during their old age. She explained that most of them were self-destructive and that Lilli's mother was probably in no danger. He probably was only a danger to himself.

Lilli filed that information away for the present time and tried to concentrate on the dilemma in her own life. Who and where was her father?

After Lilli had finished all her stories that she had learned while visiting in Otwell, Mabel began to question her about her future plans. She was shocked to hear about the disappearance of Lilli's birth father.

"What do you plan to do, Lilli?"

"I shall begin to look for him, when I can think of a plan of action. At this moment, I have no idea where to start."

The clock in the hall chimed eleven, and the women knew that it was time to go to bed. Tomorrow would be a new day, and they could discuss this project then.

Lilli went to her room and realized again that it was a solemn and peaceful place for her. Since she had slept very little the night before, Lilli fell asleep almost instantly with the plan that she would begin again in the morning. She longed to have Grayson to talk to about this new part of her life, but he was gone. Someone else shared him now, and she would need to move on with her new adventure of where George Jackson might be?

Chapter 46

Once again, the school year began. One of the first chores that faced Lilli was the stack of mail that was awaiting her in the school office. The secretary stated that the mail had continued to accumulate during the summer months. Lilli took the box of letters and put them in the back seat of her car. Lilli returned to her classroom and tried to put most of her energy into fulfilling the needs of her students. She really loved the atmosphere of the classroom although she wondered if she were teaching to the best of her ability. The gnawing mystery of her father was filed neatly in the back of her mind, and she wondered how to begin to find him, coupled with the continuing collection of mail from Bloomington, gave Lilli more to think about that she wanted to deal with at this time. The mystery of finding her father seem to be uppermost in her mind right now. She didn't seem to think of a way to look for him, since there was a huge time lapse as well as land and roads between Otwell and Evansville. Mother had only said that he rode off to the West. But where? It had been 28 years since he had made the decision to leave. Could he be somewhere near her now? A man would have to have a job to support himself. She knew that he would be working somewhere, but was it on a farm? Suppose he was no longer alive. She realized that possibility existed. She knew only one thing. She would not stop until she found him, somehow, someway.

It would soon be winter in Evansville, and school was occupying most of her time. The late fall weather meant that she and Mabel would not be sitting on the porch with their tea cups many more afternoons after school. However, as long as the sun was setting it cast a long shadow across the porch and the two women enjoyed the last vestiges of summer, even if it meant that they were bundled in sweaters.

One afternoon, just before twilight, the two of them had been swinging in the old porch swing and enjoying their tea when Lilli excused herself and went inside the house for a moment. Suddenly a tall young man and a young girl came walking up the walk to Mabel's home. He smiled at the Mabel and asked if Lilli Jackson lived at this address. Mabel was taken aback and replied that she did, in fact, live there. He asked if he could speak with her for a few moments. As he was making his request, Lilli heard a male voice and hurried back to the doorway to see what the stranger was asking of Mabel. When she stepped to the doorway, she recognized the stranger; it was Grayson. He was a mature man and more handsome than she had remembered. And, with him, was a young girl who appeared to be about 5 or 6 years old.

Lilli stepped onto the porch and asked, "How can I help you, Grayson? Why are you here? How did you find me?' And who is your partner?

Mabel was quite confused and asked how she knew this young man.

After a few minutes of introductions and explanations as to who he was, and why he was there, Mabel excused herself and left the two people together on the porch. She went indoors to prepare something for all of them to eat. She had heard the heartbreaking story of how Grayson had abandoned Lilli to marry her best friend, Vickie had been pregnant and abandoned by the father of the child. Mabel was sure that there were many years of catching up to do between the two former lovers.

Grayson began to talk in spurts about the past six years. He was quite cautious about giving too many details about the past because of exposing the facts in front of the child.

"Tell me, what is this child's name," Lilli asked.

"I am sorry to be rude," Grayson said, "her name is Amanda. She is our daughter. I brought her on this trip because her mother isn't very well, and I thought she could use the rest from the burdens of a family for a few days," he continued.

Amanda stepped to the side of the chair where Lilli was sitting, and asked, "Are you the Lilli that my mother knew when she was a little girl?"

"I am, replied Lilli, and we had many good times together."

"Will you come to see my mother; she isn't very well?"

Lilli looked to Grayson and wondered just what she should say in answer to the child's question. "Of course, I will. Sometime soon I will visit you at your home," was the only logical answer that she could give at the moment. She needed more facts about how sick Vickie was and whether or not a visit would be a good idea. Lilli put her arms around the child and pulled her to her, recognizing that she could instantly fall in love with her. She was so very beguiling.

As Lilli looked into her eyes, she thought about what a beautiful child she was. Her skin was almost transparent and resembled a cameo with a tinge of rosy cheeks. Her light brown hair framed the features of her face, and her eyes were liquid blue. Her long hair was pulled back by a wide barrette leaving her face the focal point of the entire child. She was dressed in a long pinafore in a pale pink which only accented her complexion. Lilli realized how much she looked like her mother.

Mabel reappeared at the door and announced that she had laid out the evening meal. She invited the guests in to enjoy their supper together. Grayson tried to say that he and Amanda would go to a nearby restaurant and return after dinner. Mabel would have none of that kind of excuse. Everyone would sit at the table and the meal that she had prepared.

The conversation at the dinner table was light and not very detailed. Although Lilli was 'dying' to hear about what had gone on in the life of Grayson and Vickie, she refrained from asking any questions which would not be appropriate to discuss in front of Amanda.

She filled the mealtime with conversations about her school and the visit to Otwell, leaving out the part about Father and his personality disorder. She did not mention that she had found her birth mother's grave either because it would have been too many confusing details to discuss in one evening. There would be time for that later.

After the foursome had completed their meal, Lilli took Amanda into her room and explained that she would be sleeping with her that evening. When Amanda looked around the room, she spied a picture of Lilli and Grayson. "Why do you have a picture of my daddy?" came her question.

"Oh, we went to college together many years ago. This picture was taken on the campus outside our residence hall at the college," Lillie managed to say, hoping that she did not need to go into any more details about their relationship. Amanda seemed satisfied with her explanation.

As Lilli tucked her into bed, she whispered that she was very proud of her and how grown up she seemed to be. She kissed the child and wondered if any children of her own would be as sweet and innocent as Amanda seemed to be.

Lilli walked out of her own room and slowly pulled the door shut behind her. She was hoping that she could get more information about the circumstances surrounding the 'mystery' of Vickie's illness and just why Grayson had sought her out again.

Chapter 47

As she walked back into the parlor, Lilli noticed that Mabel had refreshed their coffee and was planning to go to her room. "No, you must stay in the room with us," Lilli stated, "you are a part of this story too. I have never had secrets from you and I will not start now."

Mabel took a seat across the room from Lilli and Grayson and prepared to listen to the stories that might be revealed from the last six years.

"You know that I went to Medical School at Bloomington," began Grayson. "I graduated from there, Magma Cum Laude, and went to the University Hospital in Terre Haute for my residency. Amanda was born in Bloomington and Vickie was so proud of her. She spent all her time doting on her. It was as if Amanda was the only thing that she could hold onto. While I studied hard and tried to work a few part time jobs, Vickie was left alone most of the time. She never complained, but I guess she must have mourned for Tom. I had failed to notice that she never seemed to forget him. She never spoke his name to me."

"I took her back to Otwell one time, to see her family, but she told me later that she was very uncomfortable there. She introduced me as Amanda's father, but somehow I don't think her mother believed Vickie at all. I had to agree with Vickie, I was uncomfortable too."

141

"Her mother spent the entire weekend talking about other things that had happened in Otwell, most of which neither of us knew anything about since Vickie had been gone a long time and I had never even visited there. It was just a very strange weekend."

Grayson stopped in his story long enough to ask to have his coffee refilled, then he continued on with the story of the last few years.

"When I was accepted at the University Hospital in Terre Haute, we packed up our meager belongings and moved there. Amanda was not quite old enough to go to school, so it was a good time to move. We settled into a small house near the hospital and I began my work there. Vickie was alone again during the day, with only Amanda as a companion on many evenings. I blame myself for not being more of a husband to her; however, I tried very hard to be a father to Amanda. She is such a precious child."

Lilli and Mabel were spellbound listening to Grayson tell about his life. Lilli could not imagine how all of this could have happened without her knowledge. Then she remembered that he had written to her and she had not opened his letters. They were tucked away in a box in her room, unopened. And, she also remembered the box of unopened letters now resting on the back seat of her car. How foolish of her, she thought, now. Why was I so childish as to abandon him when he might have needed me? Then the question that begged answering now was; why was he here at this time?

Grayson continued to give the details of their move to Terre Haute and his becoming a practicing physician. He explained that he had set up a practice with another doctor in the area and had begun to develop his business.

Vickie had become a volunteer at some of the local medical facilities. She had become quite interested in the Chinese people who had come to Vigo County as part of the contingent of men who had helped to build the railroad from Evansville to Terre Haute and on to Chicago. She had befriended a few of the women who had invited her to share in their culture, Grayson explained.

"Unfortunately, for Vickie, I did not pay enough attention to her behavior at that time. After only a couple of months of her association with the Chinese women, I noticed that her behavior was becoming quite strange. She spent more and more time with them, and suddenly I realized that she was joining them in the Opium dens, smoking the stuff almost daily." With that statement, Grayson bowed his head and fought bravely not to shed more tears.

He turned to Lilli and through his liquid eyes, he said, "Lilli, she is completely wasted." She is a full blown Opium addict. She has to have the opiate more than three times a day. The effects of Opium has caused her to be misshapen and deformed. I can no longer allow Amanda to see her. I do not want her to remember her mother in this condition."

Lilli gulped back the tears that she felt when she heard Grayson describe her once best friend. She could hardly believe what she was hearing. Lilli could not picture the scene that he was describing since she had never seen such an addict.

Mabel spoke up and said that she had only read about such addictions in a magazine once. However, those people all lived in California. She stated that she didn't realize that such a malady existed in Indiana. Her thoughts were that it was only a problem in China that had manifested itself in Chinatown in California. However, she had never known Vickie, so she could not really imagine how she might have been enticed to partake of such an evil substance. With that statement, she announced that she was going to bed. It would be morning and she needed to be able to get ready for church. She turned to Grayson and told him that he was to sleep on the sofa and that she would bring him adequate quilts and a pillow for his comfort.

Grayson tried to explain that he had no intention of staying the night, but Mabel assured him that she had no intention of him leaving. That settled the matter, and she wandered off to bed.

Chapter 48

Grayson and Lilli continued to talk throughout most of the night. He explained, in a medical fashion, the prospects of Vickie ever being able to fight this addiction. She was too far gone. It pained him to explain how grotesque her body had become. He related how she had large knobs all over her body where her elbow or knee joint were supposed to be. Her face was contorted until even a close friend would have trouble identifying her.

During the time that he was talking about Vickie, Lilli had remained in the chair across the room. She did not trust herself to be near him as he related his unhappiness to her. Grayson had not stated that he was unhappy with Vickie, only that he was devastated that he had not noticed her unhappiness sooner. He seemed to carry most of the blame for her situation. And, he had a great deal of empathy for Amanda.

Finally, after several hours, Lilli stated that she had something to tell him too. She began by telling him about her visit to Mother and Father. She mentioned that she had not been back for several years. She had wrapped herself up in teaching her classes and she had little or no time for outside activities. This summer, she had decided to make the trip to Otwell driving her new car.

Lilli related to him how Father had been so belligerent and hateful to her and Mother. She couldn't understand why he didn't seem to know who she was, part of the time.

Grayson explained that it was called 'dementia' and many times older people would seem to have it. It occurred because a part of the brain cells slowly die or become dysfunctional. He continued with his explanation and told Lilli that she might have to make some arrangements for him to be cared for somewhere away from her mother. He might become dangerous to her or himself. Lilli wondered if that was already happening. She filed that information away and decided that she would think about it later.

Chapter 49

"You will never guess what I found while I was in Otwell," she began.

"I would have no way of knowing what you might have discovered," Grayson replied.

"I am not sure if you ever knew that I had a question about why my name was Jackson and my parents name was Horton. I had wondered about it for many years, but thought perhaps that was how they honored one of their family members."

"While I was in Otwell visiting, I grew a bit restless in the farmhouse and decided to venture out into the community. While I was out walking, I stopped in at the church where Vickie and I once sang in the choir. The pastor was in his study, and he heard me walking around, humming some of the old hymns. While he was telling me about the services, and how the congregation had grown, we walked out into the cemetery. I have always been fascinated by gravestones and I began reading the inscriptions on them. Can you imagine my surprise when I noticed one that said 'Lula Elayne Jackson'? Her death occurred the same day that I was born. I left the pastor standing in the cemetery and hurried back to the house. I approached Mother with my information. She hung her head and slowly told me that the woman buried in that grave was, in fact, my biological mother."

"Then, where is your father?" Grayson asked.

"No one seems to know. Mother said that when he handed me, only a few hours old, over to her, he simply said that he would be back. However, when the funeral was over, he returned to her with the key to his front door and the deed to his farm saying that he was giving them everything that he had in the entire world. He mounted his horse and rode away toward the west." Those were Mother's own words. 'He rode away toward the west'. No one has seen or heard from him since."

Grayson broke the reverie when he looked at Lilli and asked, "How do you feel about that?"

"Oh, Grayson, I shall never stop until I find him. He can't be far away. If it takes a lifetime, I will search until I find him. I want to believe that he is sorry that he gave me away. I want to feel that he has regretted his decision many times over, but can not bring himself to admit it even to himself. I know that he felt that he had no choice at the time. He thought he was unequipped to raise me on his own, and it appeared to him at the time that giving me to Mother and Dad was the thing to do. I am a 'believer' and I know that God will help me find him."

Grayson looked at the woman that he had once loved more than anything. Now, when he looked into her eyes, and could feel her pain for her lost family, he wanted to hold her in his arms and soothe her sobbing heart. However, he remembered that he had a wife, albeit one who hardly knew him. But to make a mockery of his choice to marry her to give Amanda a father forced him to remain true to Vickie.

Lilli and Grayson continued to talk about some of the events in their lives until the hall clock chimed three times indicating it was three o'clock in the morning. Lilli stood and announced that she was going to join Amanda in the bed. They could talk more after a good night's rest.

She leaned over Grayson as he was sitting on the sofa and kissed his forehead. "You are a fine man, Grayson, and I am so happy you have found me." She hurried out of the room before she changed her swift kiss on the forehead into a passionate one for the husband of her best friend.

Lilli went to her room to get some sleep. She remembered the box of unopened letters that she had stored on the top shelf of the closet and the box still resting in the back seat of her car. She glanced at the box on the shelf that seemed to be peering down at her and decided that she had already learned all that she needed to know about what might possibly be in those letters. She drifted off to sleep thinking that someday she would read them; but not tonight.

Grayson and Amanda stayed for two days with Mabel and Lilli. The foursome had a good time taking in the sights and sounds of the area. It was early fall and the weather was good. Amanda loved the trip to the zoo to see the animals but most of all she loved riding on the carousel. They ate a picnic lunch that

Mabel had prepared for them and then left the zoo area for the river's edge. Amanda was entertained by the steamboat that was going down river, and then she saw a towboat pushing a barge loaded with coal up the river. Mabel assured them that the barge was probably going to Cincinnati or maybe to Pittsburgh. No one questioned her knowledge since none of them had any better idea as to where the huge barge might be going.

As they walked around enjoying the afternoon, nothing more was said about Vickie. Since Amanda knew nothing of her mother's malady, it was not a subject to be discussed in her presence. Grayson had only told her that Vickie was in the hospital trying to get better. Because she was a child, Amanda accepted his explanation and rarely asked about her mother. Lilli realized how much she had missed Grayson since she had last seen him. It had been almost 7 years since they had graduated and he left for medical school. She had managed to keep busy with her teaching career and her life with Mabel, but it was obvious to her that she missed the camaraderie that they had once shared.

After the family had eaten their evening meal, they all sat on the porch and watched the sunset. Amanda heard a whistle that they explained was from a train hurrying through town. Lilli gave a great description of how the trains transported various materials across country. She explained how people sometimes traveled as far as from one side of the United States to the other side on a train. She wondered what they would be teaching Amanda in school in Terre Haute when she began school soon. These were elementary facts that she taught in her own classroom in Evansville.

Soon it was time to put Amanda to bed, and she gladly allowed Lilli to put her to bed. She snuggled down in the bed and put her arms around Lilli begging her to pretend that she was her mother. It was very difficult for Lilli to accept this offer. She fought back the tears but quickly agreed that they would play this game for the night. Tomorrow, she would return to Terre Haute with her father and Lilli would remain in Evansville. "You will come and visit us, won't you?" the child asked.

"Of course, I will."

"Will you come soon?"

"Perhaps I will come for the Thanksgiving holiday, if it is agreeable with your father." Amanda bounded from the bed and ran to the parlor to find Grayson. "She can come for Thanksgiving, can't she dad?" Grayson, not knowing what her question was all about, nodded his head in assent. Amanda returned to her bed and related the consent that she had received from Grayson that she should visit them during the Thanksgiving weekend. "I will try to work on that plan," Lilli stated. That is when I will not be teaching my class at school, and I will have three days to spend. I will ride the train to Terre Haute and your daddy can bring you to the train station to meet me. Would that be OK with you?"

Lilli asked the sleepy child. Before she could answer, Amanda had drifted off to sleep. Lilli went back to the front porch and stated that the child was asleep but that she had made a promise to her that she would come to Terre Haute over the Thanksgiving weekend to visit. "I will need your approval of this plan, Grayson."

"Permission granted," he replied. "I want your opinion of what you think I can do to help Vickie."

"You are the doctor, doctor. How would I know what you should do?"

"I guess I need a woman's point of view. I have never discussed Vickie's problem with her parents. They have not been in contact with her very much and so I don't really have a good relationship with them. I know they would love to see Amanda and spend time with her, but Vickie never wanted to go there after we went to Bloomington."

The night air was turning cooler and they decided to step inside and continue their conversations. Again, the two of them talked into the wee hours of the morning. It was obvious that they did not want their time together to end. However, it was clear that they both honored the fact that he was married and his wife was not present.

Morning came and the four of them enjoyed a great breakfast around the big table. Amanda was already making plans for Lilli's visit in November. Grayson loaded the car and prepared to return to his work at the hospital in Terre Haute. Life for now would continue as it had prior to his visit with his former lover. He was proud of himself for having remained a gentleman and felt confident that if he had tried to make any overtures toward Lilli, she would have rebuffed him and remained a lady. He loved her even more for that.

BACK TO GEORGE JACKSON
Chapter 50

George continued to work for C&EI railroad. He had progressed up the ladder of success by becoming a conductor, like he had only dreamed of a few years ago. He was a faithful employee and worked to become the best that he could be for the company.

He had also become a dedicated husband to Barbara whom he had married in the spring. He had lived at her house for several years and had become her lover nearly five years ago. He had proposed to her and they had discussed their 'May to November' relationship. Both of them agreed that age made no difference to them. They had developed a great family atmosphere together. George worked on her house, planted a large garden, kept the car that they had purchased in good running order and generally was a wonderful husband. Barbara had continued to keep the home fires burning and welcomed him home when he came in 'off the road' from his trips up to Chicago and home again. Their personal life had continued to be a blessing to both of them. While it may have cooled a bit with time, it still was very satisfying and rewarding. George was delighted to have such a wonderful wife after being alone so many years. It seemed like a lifetime since he had buried his sweet young bride, Lula. Only occasionally did he question himself about where his daughter Lilli might be today. When the thought of her came to his mind, he tried very hard to push it to the back of his memory and only prayed that someday he would see her again. He had no idea how he might find her unless he went back to Otwell to look for her. He had no intention of returning to his hometown because of the memories that he had there. He often thought that he had not left in the best of terms, but at the time, he felt that he had no choice.

Chapter 51

The Thanksgiving holiday was rapidly approaching. Lilli was busy working on her wardrobe to take to what she referred to as the 'big city'. Although Terre Haute was not as big as Evansville, it was a change of pace, for her and she was anxiously looking forward to her visit there. She had mixed emotions about the trip to visit Grayson. She wanted to see him again, but she wondered what she would do when she met Vickie. Would she resent her being there? Would Vickie wonder why Lilli came to visit since she hadn't been in contact with her at all since they graduated from college? Or worse yet, would she even recognize her? Grayson had told her that Vickie was very sick and that sometimes she didn't know him. Would she remember Lilli?

Finally she had all her plans made. She would leave immediately after school on Wednesday afternoon. Mabel would drive her to the station. On Sunday evening, Mabel would pick her up when her train arrived about 7:00 P.M., if it was on time. The stationmaster had told her that sometimes it ran late and it might be 8:00 before it got into the station. The women agreed to that arrangement and Lilli bought her 'roundtrip' ticket.

Wednesday finally came. Mabel packed a lunch for Lilli to eat while on the train. Lilli took the latest Charles Dickens book to read on the train before it got too dark to read. She had no idea that there would be a light over her seat on the train. This was her first train ride and she hardly knew what to do unless someone told her.

When the train sped north on the track, Lilli watched as the farm fields flew by the window. She saw barns, horses, chickens, and even a few sheep. Instantly, she was reminded of life in Otwell. Strange how she never enjoyed living there, but when she thought about it, she had to admit that perhaps she did miss the leisure lifestyle that small town people lived. And then she thought about Mother and Dad. Was he treating Mother better? Or was he getting worse. She made a mental note that she would need to visit there again, soon.

As the train rattled on up the track, it seemed to lull Lilli to sleep. She laid her head back on the seat and fell asleep. The next thing that she knew was that the conductor was shouting out the station of Terre Haute, Indiana. She was startled to realize that she had slept most of the way and probably would have gone on to Chicago if the conductor had not jostled her shoulder to awaken her. She gathered her bags and left the train when it arrived at the station. She was hoping that Grayson would be there to meet her since she didn't know how to find him if he were not there.

She need not have worried about his not being there to greet her because as she stepped onto the steps to leave the train, Amanda came running across the waiting area and threw her arms around Lilli as a greeting. Grayson was not far behind but he was carrying a bouquet of flowers which he presented to her. "What did I do to deserve these?" she asked.

"It's a gift for you," Amanda replied. "We wanted to make you feel welcome to our town."

"You make me feel very welcome, Amanda, and I thank you both for your thoughtfulness," Lilli said, hiding her tears as she spoke. She had never had such a welcome from anyone.

Grayson took Lilli and Amanda to a nearby restaurant for their evening meal. "I'm not much of a cook, so we probably will eat a few meals in restaurants while you are here," he said. Amanda chimed in with her comments. "He is not a good cook, and I can only make oatmeal. I didn't think you would want oatmeal for dinner after your train ride."

"I can eat anything, Amanda; when I was in college, I didn't have much money and I ate a lot of oatmeal and boiled eggs."

"I hope you didn't eat them together. They sound yucky to me."

"If you two will quit talking about oatmeal, I will treat you both to a nice meal in this restaurant," Grayson said. However, if you prefer oatmeal….

"Stop it daddy, I don't even like oatmeal. Can I have fried chicken?"

"You may have whatever you like tonight because we have a guest, but remember that you must clean your plate, and you must mind your manners"

"I will make you proud of me, Daddy, just wait and see."

The party of three went to dinner and enjoyed a meal over conversations about the hospital where Grayson was a resident physician. Amanda chimed in with a question occasionally but realized that most of the topics that they were discussing were basically adult talk.

They returned home and settled in for an evening of conversation. After about an hour, Grayson informed Amanda that it was her bedtime. "May I sleep with Lilli?" she asked. Before Grayson could answer, Lilli spoke up to agree that she would love to have Amanda as a bed-partner, just like they had done when she visited in Evansville. "I will share my teddy-bear with you," Amanda proclaimed.

"I love teddy-bears, Amanda, and I will snuggle up with it, if it should happen to stray out of your arms while you are asleep," Lilli responded, and then she took Amanda by the hand and led her to the room where the two of them would be sleeping. After a good night kiss and a few brief bedtime prayers, she tucked the child in the bed and realized how sad it was that she didn't have a mother to look after her.

Lilli returned to the living room where Grayson had poured them a small glass of wine. "I don't dare drink that, Lilli said, or I will fall asleep instantly." I have never been able to drink wine."

"I don't want you to fall asleep instantly, Grayson

said, I think we have a lot to talk about before you fall asleep."

The two people talked for several hours about their lives. Lilli admitted to Grayson that she had never opened his letters. She confessed that she had been so hurt by his choice to marry Vickie that she didn't want to hear about their lives together.

"You should have opened them, he said, I explained a lot of things in those letters."

"I really don't want to hear about all that now," she replied. "We need to deal with the present. I want to go to the Sanitarium to see Vickie. Can we arrange that? And, what about Amanda? I know that she doesn't know where her mother is."

"Tomorrow is Thanksgiving day. We will eat here at home. I really am a reasonably good cook, and I will prepare a good meal for us. We will spend more time together, maybe go to the park if it isn't too cold, and enjoy time with Amanda. Then on Friday, I will take her to the baby-sitter's house and she will stay there while we visit Vickie. Then on Friday evening, we might even go to the movie with Amanda."

"I believe that you have thought this through, haven't you?"

"It's not every day that I have a guest to visit us in our home. I want to be a good host."

"You are a good host, Grayson, and a good father to a beautiful child." Lilli could not go any further in this conversation. It was just too painful for her to mention the life that she once had with him. If she began to think about their future that had been thwarted in its infancy, it would bring on a barrage of tears. She was very guarded in her response to his conversations. She was well aware that he was still a married man.

Chapter 52

Grayson prepared a delightful feast to celebrate the Thanksgiving holiday. The three of them ate baked chicken and all the trimmings. Lilli smiled to think that she would not have been able to prepare such feast on her own. If a man had graduated medical school then perhaps that also gave him the skill to bake a chicken.

The weather for the holiday was perfect and the party of three went for a walk in the park. Amanda was full of conversation and continued to occupy all the attention.

In the evening, they ate the leftovers from the noon meal and consumed the rest of the pumpkin pie. Soon it was bedtime for Amanda, and, accompanied by her teddy-bear, she headed off to bed. Of course, she insisted on having Lilli tuck her in the bed and help her with her bedtime prayers.

When Lilli returned to the living room, Grayson had made a place for her on the sofa with him. He wanted her nearby. She wasn't sure that she could control her emotions, but it was evident that she would have to try very hard to remain a neutral force.

"I am not trying to confuse you, Lilli. Please hear me out. There never was any doubt that I was in love with you from the time that we were together in college. I have never forgotten you and I am still in love with you. And, having you here with me makes it even harder for me. I made a conscious decision to help someone in need at the time. I had no way of knowing that she would destroy herself. Please, understand how hard it is for me, a medical doctor, to see my wife as an Opium addict and incurable. I want to help her now, but I can't seem to find a way. And, I have done all that I can do for her. I am raising her daughter for her and trying to protect her from the vices of her mother. Tell me, what would you have me do now?"

Lilli did not expect to get such a confession from Grayson. She had to struggle to keep her emotions in check as he was talking about their life and the life he had devoted to Vickie.

She stood to her feet and smiled down on Grayson as he was reclining on the sofa. It was hard for her to speak, but she knew that it was time to make a difference in his life.

"I know, Grayson, that you have done all that you can do for her. Perhaps this started in the very beginning, when she should have faced her adversity alone and not expected you to help her hide the truth. Or maybe we are all to blame for not helping her to understand the deceit of Tom Howard. And maybe I am at fault for not opening your letters where I would have discovered your discontent and her addiction. But it is always easy to 'second guess' what 'might have been.' The truth is that she is very sick; you are working very hard to support yourself and her child, and we are helpless to do much to save her."

"In answer to your question about what do I think you should do to help her? I will be better prepared to answer that question after I see her tomorrow." With that statement, Lilli stood and kissed his forehead and hurried to her bedroom to sleep with Amanda next to her in bed.

Chapter 53

The morning light was streaming through the sheer curtains in the bedroom casting an eerie glow over the room. The cheery wallpaper reminded her of her old bedroom in Otwell. She realized that the trend was the same whether it was Otwell or Terre Haute, wallpaper was always used to brighten a room and to add a touch of color to the surroundings.

It was time to get up, she thought. She noticed that Amanda had already dressed and was probably in the kitchen with Grayson. She hurriedly dressed, pulled her hair up in a bun, and joined the two of them in the kitchen. "Where's my coffee?" she asked.

"Morning makes her grouchy, Daddy."

"Oh, Amanda, everyone is grouchy until they get their coffee."

"Let's just humor her, and pour her a cup."

"I resent that remark," Lilli chided. "I am not grouchy." Then she turned and hugged the child whispering in her ear that she sure looked sweet in her pinafore.

The three of them finished off the breakfast that Grayson had prepared and hurriedly dressed for their day out. Amanda was going to the home of the lady that would entertain her for the day. Grayson and Lilli had plans to visit the hospital where he worked and to see the sights of the city. At least, that was the story that was discussed at the table. Amanda was not to know that Grayson and Lilli were going to the Sanitarium where Vickie was a patient.

Terre Haute was not a particularly beautiful city. It had many industries that continued to belch and puff dirty smoke into the atmosphere. No one seemed concerned about this condition and so it was allowed to continue. Grayson explained that there were many coalmines in the area as well and they continued to leave gaping holes in the 'once fertile' farm lands. All of these conditions made the city appear dirty and smoky.

The hospital where Grayson worked was a modern looking building which appeared to be able to handle a vast number of patients. He explained to Lilli that he could not take her inside since his 'fellow' doctors would not understand the situation of him and another woman. Lilli smiled and agreed that he didn't need another problem in his life.

Grayson drove over to the Sanitarium to visit Vickie. It was a grey overpowering building obviously in need of some repair. When the two of them started up the steps to the building, she noticed that they were quite dilapidated. But the exterior was nothing compared to what she would witness on the inside.

As the two of them entered the lobby, she noticed that the odor of ether, antiseptic, and urine were all mixed to cause a disgusting insult to her nostrils. The nurse on duty was obese, terse, and impatient with them stating that the person they wanted to see was down the hall and in the ward on the left. Obviously Grayson had been there before and was aware of the conditions; conditions that were quite disturbing to Lilli.

When they entered the ward where Vickie was, Lilli noticed that there were four beds in the room. The room was dirty, smelly, and dingy. The windows were covered by torn curtains and the glass was so dirty, that the sunlight would never be able to penetrate the filth on the glass to add any brightness to the room. In each of the beds was a person who was in various stages of disability. Lilli soon found which bed was Vickie's since her name in bold letters was painted right on the end of the bed. But when she focused on the occupant, she could hardly control her emotions.

Lilli walked over to Vickie and leaned over to hug her. She still loved her friend, even though she could hardly look at her. The Opium had taken its toll on her wonderful friend. Her face was covered in large growths. One almost covered her left eye, causing her to tilt her head to see from the right eye. There were nodules growing on her scalp, arms, and fingers preventing them from bending. Her limbs were distorted into unrecognizable shapes. Her hair was matted and stuck to her head. And, it was obvious that she was unable to walk. Lilli wondered if she knew her.

Vickie tilted her head and squinted her one eye. "Do I know you?" she asked.

"Vickie, it is me, Lilli."

It took a few seconds for the message to reach Vickie's mind. Tears began to fall from her eyes, and she put her gnarled hands over her face. She hung her head and began to shake violently. Then she pulled the filthy cover over her head and slid down in the bed.

"She doesn't want to talk to us," Grayson said.

"She does this to me each time that I visit."

Lilli turned and walked through the door, glancing back at the once beautiful girlfriend that she had known since childhood. She could hardly control her tears as she entered the hall. By the time she reached the lobby, she was moving as fast as she could go, trying to reach the street before she collapsed in uncontrollable tears. "Oh, Grayson, I can hardly stand this. How could this have happened to her? She was so vibrant and happy when we started college. I can only imagine how this insidious disease could consume such a wonderful person. Her life is over, isn't it? She can never recover, can she? And this addiction will take her life, won't it?"

Grayson put his arms around her shoulders and slowly explained that the addiction was not reversible with the medicine of the day. And, if she continues to participate in using Opium, it will take her life. They do not have many remedies to stop the addiction and the caretakers continue to give her more to keep her under control. If she isn't using the drug, she becomes very unruly as do the others in the room. They have no other way to take care of them. It is sad, but that is the life these girls have chosen, not knowing what the outcome would be for them. The growths and nodules that you see on her body are the results of an infection that she apparently got from Tom Howard. She may have begun to use Opium as a way of hiding the evidence of Syphilis that she had contracted from him. He was so promiscuous; I am sure that he didn't even realize that he had such a disease. Regardless of where he got it, or when it was transferred to her remains a mystery to me. I only know that she began to show signs of the disease shortly after the birth of Amanda.

Lilli and Grayson stopped in a local café to enjoy an afternoon lunch. They continued to discuss Vickie and what he could possibly do to help her. Their consensus of opinion was that nothing either of them could do would help. Then, the conversation turned to lighter things as they began to discuss the hospital workings and, then to Lilli's school classroom. Finally, Lilli shared with Grayson her life with Mabel. She had been like a second mother to her. She had previously shared the story of how she had found out who her natural born mother really was. And how her endless search for her natural father had never left her mind, but that she was stymied as to where she should begin to look for him. She only knew that his name was George Jackson.

The two of them had an afternoon of conversation that had been long in coming. And, it was clear to both of them that the feelings between them were mutual. Lilli had a continuing concern that Grayson might be carrying the latent disease of syphilis that he might have contracted from Vickie. However, she chose not to mention it to him. It was something that she would need to ponder for a while.

. Soon it was time to get Amanda and return home. Lilli needed to get her things ready to make the trip back to Evansville the next morning.

Chapter 54

Early the next morning Lilli loaded all her luggage into the car and prepared to go to the train station. She had purchased a large vase to take to Mabel and she had carefully packed it in another container. She had reserved a book to read on the train as it steamed along on the way home. Amanda had baked some cookies and she put a few in a bag for her to enjoy on the train. Everything seemed in order for her to head home. Leaving had not been easy for her. She really wanted Grayson to beg her to stay, even though it would be impossible. She had a class to teach, and a life to live without Grayson. And, he had a life to live with Amanda and Vickie. He had many decisions to make.

Lilli boarded the train after saying her goodbyes to Amanda and Grayson. She used her linen handkerchief to wipe the tears from the eyes of Amanda. She hugged her and kissed her several times and told her how much she had enjoyed having her as a sleeping partner. She turned to Grayson and allowed him to hug her rather romantically. She looked into his eyes and acknowledged his hidden message. Then she rushed up the steps of the train without looking back. She quickly found her seat and slid over to the window seat to wave goodbye to the two of them. When an elderly man came down the aisle, she stood up and offered him the seat by the window. He had relatives to wave goodbye to also, as the train was leaving the station.

She settled into her seat and retrieved her book from her bag. She was certain that she would get engrossed in it and the time would pass more quickly. She just needed to think about something other than the past three days.

The conductor came down the aisle taking tickets. She dug around in her bag and located the return trip ticket that she had purchased in Evansville. She was preparing to hand the ticket to the conductor when she glanced up into his face. He seemed so friendly. Right now, she needed a friend. Instantly her eyes were drawn to his name tag. Her heart nearly stopped. The tag said: G. Jackson. "Mr. Jackson," she stammered, "have you ever lived in Otwell, Indiana?" Lilli shocked herself at her presence of mind to ask such a question of a perfect stranger. The words had simply tumbled from her lips. Surely, she thought, I should not be so brazen as to Inquire Into this man's past. Before she could apologize for her Impetuous question, the man focused his stare on her.

George looked down into the eyes of a beautiful girl, but more than that, she was an almost perfect replica of a woman that he had been married to many years before, named Lula. "Why yes, my dear, I did live in Otwell, a long time ago. Why do you ask?" George did not dare to allow his emotions to cloud his judgment. He was not sure if he wanted to believe what appeared to be his daughter.

"My name is Lilli. I believe you are my father. Only recently did I discover that my mother apparently died in childbirth and that my father left Otwell. I hope that I am not too bold In asking you the question of your previous residence."

George listened carefully to what she was saying, and he knew that she was telling the truth. He often wondered about his daughter and now she was sitting right in front of his eyes. What could he say to her? How could he possibly explain his actions? How did she feel about him? She might have lots of questions but he had not given enough thought to what he would say to her if he ever saw her. He wanted to talk to Barbara now. She would know what to tell him to say to his baby girl who was now a grown woman.

"I have to take the other tickets on the train and then I will come back and talk to you," George said. "I really want to visit with you. We can go into the dining car and talk, privately." He turned and went on down the aisle leaving Lilli in a fog. She wasn't sure what she wanted to say to him, but now, she had a few minutes to think about it. George had hurriedly left her because he had to think about what he needed to tell her about his actions on the day that she was born.

George walked on through the rest of the cars and gathered the tickets from the other passengers. He seemed a bit boggled by the events of the last thirty minutes. He had often wanted to know where Lilli was, but now that she was right here In front of him, he didn't know what he should say to her. It was obvious that she didn't need his financial support. She was well dressed and appeared to be successful. Where did she live? Her ticket was from Evansville, Indiana but she had boarded the train in Terre Haute. He wondered why?

The tickets were all collected and George returned to the seat where Lilli was seated. He tapped her on the shoulder and motioned for her to follow him into the dining car. As soon as they were seated a black man stepped up to the table and asked if they would like coffee. George quickly ordered coffee for both of them, then he turned to Lilli to see if he could satisfy his curiosity of what had taken place her life. And he was certain that she might continue to wonder what had happened in his life.

Lilli began by telling her father that she had gone to college in Evansville, that she was a teacher and teaching in a school near where she lived. She mentioned the trip to Otwell the previous summer where she discovered her mother's gravestone. She touched on the condition of the Horton's and how Father had been mistreating Mother. She pointed out that a friend who was a doctor mentioned that sometimes those things happen when a person gets older and it is called dementia. Lilli continued on in telling the highpoints of her life but she conveniently left out a lot of the details.

George leaned across the table and took Lilli's hands in his. "Lula would be very proud of you. She was only a child herself and certainly not equipped to be a mother. Her death took me by surprise, and I had no idea how to cope with it. I am so sorry to tell you that I had no reason to leave you with the Horton's except that I was afraid. I didn't know how to take care of a baby. My farm was not doing well, and I was convinced that I could not farm and raise a baby too. The Horton's seemed like a good solution to the problem that I was facing and I gave them everything that I had; my farm, my home, and my newborn baby. I never intended to abandon you. I only wanted to make sure that you would be taken care of if I wasn't there to raise you. How can you ever forgive me for what I did back then?"

Big tears were forming in her eyes as Lilli began to envision a young man with a child-like wife who had just died giving birth to a baby. Naturally he felt that he had no other choice than to give the baby to a willing mother.

"Please understand, Mr. Jackson, that I forgive you. I have tried many times to envision what you were thinking at the time. I know that your decision to act as you did had to be out of desperation. I could never blame you. I was raised in a good home and given all the opportunities that any young girl in Otwell ever had."

"Mother never talked about you at all. In fact, until I discovered my real mother's grave-stone, she had never mentioned your name. As I was growing up in

Otwell, it was always a mystery as to why my name was Jackson and their name was Horton. No one ever explained it to me."

"Where are you living now, Lilli?"

"I live in an apartment in Evansville. My landlady is my best friend and we are a good match. I live near my school, but I recently bought a car so that I can drive to school if I choose to. I am a teacher of young children in the public school system. It is a job that I really love."

"After I left Otwell, I had a very difficult time trying to find a job," George began. "When the war came, I was too old to become a soldier. Then someone told me about the railroad where I might get a job. I had first applied for work on the river loading barges, but I was hired by the railroad and it is a much better job. I have worked my way up to become the conductor. I make enough money to support me and my wife."

"I would like you to meet my wife, Barbara. We live in Vincennes. You would like her, Lilli, she is a very nice person who takes very good care of me. Please promise me that you will come to Vincennes and visit us sometime soon. I can get you a pass so that you can ride the train anytime that you would like to come and visit." George thought that this was the only thing that he had to offer his baby girl at this time. He wanted to ask her to call him 'Dad', but he was too ashamed. He hoped that he would have the opportunity to discuss how she would address him In the future.

The two strangers who were really daughter and father continued talking for about an hour. Finally George stated that he needed to get back to work. They would be pulling into a station soon and he had obligations that he had to do when they were in a station.

Lilli returned to her seat with more information than she could have ever imagined would occur as a result of on a trip to Terre Haute. Not only did she see her friend in a frightful condition, and she had found her father. That was almost more than she could handle at the moment. She would like to be able to discuss this latest development with Grayson, but he was not near her. He was already back at work at the hospital in Terre Haute.

As the train rumbled on toward Evansville, she lay back in her seat and tried to assimilate all the news that she had. Slowly she drifted off to sleep and had to be awakened when the train was pulling into the station in Evansville. She looked up to see her father tugging at her sleeve telling her that the train would soon be there and that she would need to get her bags. He smiled down at her and again asked her to make a time when she would meet with him again. "I just don't want to lose you again, Lilli. Please promise me that you will come back and see me soon."

Lilli looked into his eyes and saw the pain he was feeling at the thought of having to give her up, again. She saw that he was very contrite for his past actions, but she wasn't sure how or when she would be able to meet him again. "Oh, yes," she said, "I promise that I will see you again, very soon."

She left the train and never looked back. She saw Mabel waiting just inside the station door. Lilli took off running as fast as she could and she was shouting over and over for anyone to hear; "I found him, I found him." No one paid any attention until she was within shouting distance of Mabel. "I found him," she repeated. Mabel rushed to her side and asked just who she was talking about. "I found my father," she said. "He is the conductor on the train. I talked with him. He knew who I was. Oh, Mabel, it was wonderful to see him. Now I know who my real father is and where he is."

The ride back to her apartment was noisy with the two women chattering like two magpies on a branch. Lilli was so excited to talk about having met George. She needed to tell Mabel every detail of their conversations.

When they reached the house, it was too cold to sit on the porch, so they took their teacups and settled in the parlor for more talk. Lilli began to tell Mabel about her experience of seeing Vickie. She described what she had seen from the abominable filth in the Sanitarium to the condition of the patients. She also told Mabel that Grayson had said that the caretakers usually gave the patients more of the addictive drugs to make them more controllable. The nurses would be unable to handle the patients if they were withdrawing from the drugs; so they continued to keep them drugged. "Oh, Mabel it was just horrendous to see my once best friend in that condition. I think she knew who I was but she was too humiliated to see me. She acknowledged me in a fleeting glance but made no effort to try to talk to me." Lilli left out the part about Vickie's having contracted syphilis from Tom Howard. She didn't think it should be a part of the information that she was imparting to Mabel. She still had a lingering doubt about whether or not Grayson might be infected, too.

Mabel listened to Lilli's stories but did not ask any questions. She really wanted to ask about her relationship with Grayson but she refrained. She could see that Lilli was struggling with all these events that had happened all at one time. Mabel knew that when she had a solution to any one of them, that she would share with her what decision she had made. Her discovery of her father was the biggest shock of the trip. Mabel wondered if she would try to establish further contact with him.

Chapter 55

Lilli returned to school on Monday morning. Somehow she felt that she had been gone for a year. She had experienced more things in those last three days than she could have expected to discover in a lifetime. She had settled, in her mind that Vickie was someone whom she could not change. Vickie would remain a problem for Grayson. She could not help him make any decisions regarding her. She mourned for Amanda who was such a bright child, but had no mother. Lilli had a few such children in her classes, and it was always hard for them to adjust to other students and even more disturbing, it seemed harder for them to learn. But, she also had to decide that she couldn't help Grayson with that problem either. She would simply have to put the two of them out of her mind, at least for now.

She continued to think about her father. She wasn't sure that she was ready to establish a relationship with him at this time either. Although he was her biological father, she was having a hard time trying to look at him in that role. He had not told her how he would like to be addressed: dad? father? Mr. Jackson? She had never known him as a father figure and for now she would just accept him as the conductor on the C&EI train.

Occasionally a thought would creep into her mind about the Horton's. Mother was almost being held captive by Father in Otwell. She wondered if Mother were in mortal danger of him doing serious harm to her.

At that moment she decided that when spring came she would make another trip to Otwell to see how she was faring. Besides, she needed to tell her that she had found George Jackson. Suddenly she realized that she had even admitted to herself that she wasn't calling him 'father' yet.

The first three days back at school helped Lilli focus on her position of teacher and leader for little children. She managed to file away in her subconscious all the events that had taken place over the Thanksgiving weekend. Soon, she was planning for the Christmas pageant at school that she would need to have ready in about three weeks.

Lilli knew that winter was just around the corner. She always put her car in the garage before the bad weather arrived. She was not interested in trying to learn to drive in ice and snow. She had to get her winter clothes ready to wear to school when it was cold. All these mundane chores kept her from thinking about the other things that had taken place during her life in the last month.

Chapter 56

Shortly after she had again begun her classes at school, she received a letter from Grayson. This time she decided to open the letter, but not during school hours. She slipped the envelope in her purse and decided that she would read it in the privacy of her room after she had shared her dinner with Mabel. She didn't want to explain its contents to Mabel in case it might be it were bad news. She was hoping it was personal, and if it were, she wouldn't want to share it at all.

Lilli hurried home from school and rattled on and on about the pageant that she was helping the students prepare for the holiday season. There would be a program at the school for all the parents to attend to watch their children perform their best.

As soon as dinner was over, Lilli feigned fatigue and went immediately to her room. She could hardly wait to open the letter from Grayson. She was surprised that she had not had the same feelings of anticipation when she had received the other letters, which were still hidden away in the wooden box in her drawer. She tore open the envelope and began to read his words:

Dearest Lilli:

I enjoyed your visit so much and Amanda is still talking about you each day. She has really grown to love you in such a short time. I am sure it is because she needs a mother so badly. I don't know how I will ever explain to her what has really happened to her real mother.

The real reason for this letter is to ask if I could bring Amanda and visit with you over the Christmas holidays. I can get a few days off and it would be so nice to be with you at that time. Amanda has so few opportunities to have a real Christmas, and I am sure that you could help her get in the spirit of the holidays.

I hope you don't think me too bold to invite myself to visit. I will make arrangements at a local boarding house if you think that I should. Please let me know as soon as possible so that I can arrange my schedule here at the hospital.

Love always,
Grayson

Lilli fairly flew out of her room and knocked on Mabel's door. "I have something to ask you, Mabel. I hope that you weren't sleeping."

Mabel opened the door and the two women returned to the parlor to share their usual cup of tea. Mabel wondered why Lilli had gone to her room so quickly after dinner. Now she was going to find out.

"I have a letter from Grayson," Lilli began. "He wants to visit us again over the Christmas holidays, if that is agreeable with you. He said that he thought Amanda would enjoy a busy holiday season with us rather than being in Terre Haute, alone. He also stated that he would stay in a boarding house if you felt it would be too much for him to be here for a few days. What do you think?"

Mabel smiled and knew how much it would mean to Amanda to have a family celebration; but she wasn't fooled by Lilli's sly way of stating that she would love to have Grayson here for the holidays.

"Of course, they are welcome. We can plan a lot of events while they are here. And, you have a lot of things to tell him. He doesn't know that you have found George Jackson, does he?"

"No, Mabel, I haven't had the opportunity to write to him since returning from my trip to Terre Haute. It would be difficult to write it all down, since I am still trying to sort it all out in my own mind. It all happened so quickly, that I am wondering into what part of my life my own father might fit.

"You need to write to him immediately and tell him that you are looking forward to having a Christmas with the two of them here."

Lilli hurriedly finished her tea and returned to her room to write the letter to Grayson. She could hardly believe that she was so much involved in her life with him again. After all, he was still a married man even though his wife was disabled. She pondered what she should say to him when she finally wrote the letter. While she was reclining in the bed and thinking about what she wanted to write, she fell sound asleep. It was morning when she smelled their breakfast being cooked and could hear Mabel preparing their morning coffee. It took a few minutes for her to bring her mind around the fact that she had slept through the night with most of her clothes on. She smiled to herself when she realized that she must have been exhausted from all the excitement that she had experienced over the last few days. Her letter to Grayson would have to wait one more day.

Chapter 57

Plans were in full force for the upcoming Christmas holidays. The children in Lilli's class were practicing very hard in preparation for the day that their parents would attend and watch them perform the Christmas story. She was working long hours trying to make everything perfect for them.

Mabel was working on their celebration at home that was to take place when Grayson and Amanda were to arrive. It seemed like there was no free time for anyone at this point in their plans. Grayson was scheduled to arrive on Saturday before Christmas and would spend the weekend with them, then return to Terre Haute by the following Wednesday. It seemed like a short visit, but Lilli didn't complain. She was so anxious to see him again. She was hoping that he would tell her what he had decided to do about Vickie when he was visiting her this time. Her guilt of yearning for the companionship of a married man was taking its toll on her mental picture. She wanted him so badly, but at the same time, she knew it was wrong of her to wish such a final blow to Vickie. All the outside events that were taking place at this time kept her from 'beating herself' over this dilemma.

The school pageant was to be held on Friday prior to Grayson's arrival. Lilli was glad that one of her projects would be over by the time he arrived so that she would have more time to spend with him and

Amanda.

Mabel had prepared enough cookies and candy for the holidays that Lilli was sure that she would gain about 10 pounds from over-eating. There was to be a ham and a baked chicken. Mabel would make the usual chicken and dumplings, which had always been Lilli's favorite. She wasn't sure if Grayson and Amanda enjoyed that dish, but she was convinced that they would like one or the other of the two meat choices.

All the plans were finalized, and the pageant went off without a 'hitch'. Lilli became the 'rising star' at her school since all of the parents were well pleased with the performance of their children. Her principal complimented her profusely for such a fine job which she had done with her students.

Lilli returned home and began to make preparations for the visit from Grayson. She was very excited over the fact that he was coming. She was certainly hoping that he would have a solution to his problem. She and Mabel discussed the final touches to their celebration as they shared their afternoon tea. Outside, the weather was beginning to become blustery. It was bound to be cold for the next few days, and Lilli hated the wind. She didn't want it to be windy during their visit since she and Mabel had planned a lot of outdoor activities for all of them to participate in over the weekend.

Saturday morning came and it was going to be a long day since Lilli would have to wait for Grayson to drive down from Terre Haute. She expected him to arrive around dinner time, just before dark.

While she was finishing the last few details of the presents that she had purchased for Amanda, there was a knock on the door. She turned to Mabel and asked if she were expecting anyone to come this early in the day. Mabel assured her that she had no idea who might be at the door. When she opened the door, there stood a uniformed officer. Upon closer scrutiny, Lilli realized that he was a Sheriff's deputy. The patch on his shoulder said he was from Pike County, Indiana. Instantly, she knew that he was from Otwell. Her heart sank at the prospect that something was wrong there.

"Are you the daughter of the Horton's?" he asked looking past Mabel and addressing Lilli.

"Well, yes, I am. What is wrong, officer?"

"May I come in?" he asked, it's cold out here and I wouldn't want to make your house cold."

Mabel began to apologize for her lack of good manners, and she immediately ushered him to the parlor.

"Miss Horton," he began, and Lilli did not correct the error of her name. "There has been a terrible accident at their farm. I don't know when you saw them last, but Mr. Horton has not been well for a long time. He has not been himself. According to the neighbors, he has accused your mother of many things. He has apparently beaten her on numerous occasions. He also has wandered away from home several times and your mother has had to look for him even into the night. It appears that he has broken much of the furniture and dishes in the house in his violent rages."

Lilli dropped her head when she heard all these stories. She remembered that he had mistreated Mother when she was visiting there. She looked at the officer and said, "Continue with your story. I was aware of his uncontrollable temper. Has he disappeared?"

"No, my dear, the deputy stated, I am afraid it is much more serious than that. It appears that your father had stoked up the fire in the old cook stove but forgot to shut the damper on the flue. The stove overheated in the night and set the wall behind the cook stove on fire. The fire raged out of control while the two of them were asleep. When the neighbors discovered the house on fire, it was too late to save either of them. The house was enveloped in flames and the firemen could not enter the burning building to try to save them. They appeared to have burned to death in their sleep.

"Oh, my God," Lilli screamed. "How can that be? How do you know that it happened that way.

The deputy began to explain the circumstances that appeared to have happened.

"When did this happen?" Lilli asked.

Lilli was trying to get her thoughts together and make intelligent inquiries. "What am I to do now?"

"It took us a few days to find you. No one in Otwell knew exactly where you were, but Vickie's mother and father knew that you were in Evansville. We contacted the college and they followed up with where you were."

"Their bodies are at the funeral home in Otwell awaiting your disposition. Since it appears that you are their only heir, it will be necessary for you to make arrangements to bury them. Since it is Saturday, it will be Monday before anything can be done. The neighbors are attending to the farm animals. At this time, the decisions are all going to be yours to make."

The Sheriff's Deputy rose and shook hands with Mabel and Lilli and proceeded to leave. He stopped to express his condolences. "They were a fine family," he stated, "and I doubt that anyone knew that your father was having troubles." Many people would have stepped forward and helped them if they had known there was a need."

"They were very private people," Lilli stated. "I doubt that Mother had ever told anyone that Father was mistreating her. I doubt that he even knew that he had not attended to the stove properly. I am so sorry. They didn't deserve this kind of death."

The deputy was gone and Lilli turned to Mabel and collapsed in a torrent of tears. She sat in the chair and continued to cry uncontrollably stating that she blamed herself for not having done more to help them.

"You can't blame yourself, Lilli. They would not want you to hold yourself accountable for their actions. Your father was ill and no one seems to understand that kind of illness. Your mother was just an innocent victim. God understands these situations better than we do. I think you need to leave this problem with Him." Mabel walked to the side of the chair and knelt down, taking Lilli's hand in hers. "Let's pray," she said. "God will take care of this problem for you." Then Mabel began to pray for the victims and for Lilli. Suddenly Lilli was transported back to the little church by the graveyard in Otwell where she had spent her youth. She understood that what Mabel was saying was the truth. She bowed her head and prayed with the woman who had become like a mother to her.

Chapter 58

No sooner had the two women ended their prayer when a knock came to the door again. Lilli ran to her room to try to make her eyes lose their redness, knowing that the knock was Grayson. Mabel answered the door and welcomed their long awaited guests. Amanda hugged Mabel and asked for Lilli at about the same time that she emerged from her room.

Mabel took Amanda outside for a walk while Lilli explained to Grayson what had happened in Otwell. He could hardly believe the story that she was telling. He wrapped his arms around Lilli in an effort to comfort her. She cried into the hollow of his shoulder as he whispered into her ear that everything would be fine in a few days. He would go with her to Otwell on Monday to finalize the services if Mabel would keep Amanda. Before Lilli could respond, he kissed her very passionately and told her that he loved her very much. Those words caused Lilli to break into a torrent of tears again. "I know, Grayson, and I love you too, but it isn't good right now. We have decisions to make before we can do anything else. Right now, I must deal with the problems in Otwell. That is, right after we have Christmas right here in Evansville with Amanda and Mabel."

Mabel and Amanda returned almost as quickly as the two lovebirds had expressed their love for each other. Mabel hurried to the kitchen to put their food on the table. Grayson went to the kitchen to help her while Lilli and Amanda renewed their cozy friendship. While he was in the kitchen, he thanked Mabel for being such a strong influence on Lilli. She smiled and assured him that Lilli was the daughter that she had never had.

There were still a lot of stories to be told, but for now, the four people were going to enjoy their evening meal before it was stone cold. The festivities would come later and then the revelations of the return train trip from Terre Haute to Grayson that had surprised, even Lilli.

Chapter 59

Lilli began to tell Grayson about her discovery of her biological father on the train as she was returning from Terre Haute. He listened and seemed to be amazed that such a discovery could happen in such an unusual way. Lilli expressed the fact that she wasn't sure just how she felt about any possible involvement with George Jackson. But she was sure that she needed to inform him of the Horton's deaths, but she didn't know how to go about it. Perhaps she would figure out a way to do that through the railroad. She filed that information away in the back of her mind since she wanted to have a good time while Grayson was here.

The Christmas holiday that Mabel and Lilli had planned took place on Sunday. It was only slightly foreshadowed by the horror that had occurred in Otwell. Mabel insisted that it be put aside until after the Christmas festivities were over. The foursome went to church with Mabel and then enjoyed a wonderful dinner at home. Soon after the dinner feast, they began to open gifts. Lilli had purchased a beautiful doll for Amanda. The doll was a German made porcelain doll with eyes that opened and closed. She had natural looking blond hair. Mabel had been busy making a wardrobe of clothes for the doll. Amanda could hardly believe her good fortune and she immediately named the doll Lilli-Mabel. "I shall call her 'Lillimab'" she said as she hugged it to her breast. She loved the doll and carried it around all day. She brought an extra chair to the table and propped the doll in the chair so that it could be considered a guest at the table as they had their afternoon tea.

Grayson had brought a lovely scarf for Mabel to wear with her winter coat. He presented Lilli with a diamond and ruby brooch that he proceeded to pin on her sweater. While he was pinning the brooch on her, he was gazing into her eyes and saying softly that good times were ahead for them. Lilli had to fight back the tears. She didn't think that she could handle many more traumas in her life at this time. She, then, presented him with a fine sweater that she had purchased at a local dry goods store.

The holidays were a wonderful diversion for the problems at hand. After everyone had gone to bed, Grayson and Lilli began to discuss what should be done about her problems in Otwell. Lilli now owned a small farm with land on two sides of the road. She would need to get someone to farm the land and to tend to the animals or she would have to sell it. At this time the country was experiencing a depression, and she was sure that there would not be a buyer for either the land or the house. She wasn't even sure if the Horton's had money enough to bury them or not. But, Grayson assured her that he would pay for those expenses and any money that they might have had, she would need to use for other expenses associated with the farm.

Around 11:00 p.m. the two of them decided that

they had discussed enough for one day. Lilli allowed Grayson to kiss her again, then she quickly slipped off to her room, leaving him to sleep on the sofa. She glanced at the sleeping beauty in her bed and realized that she was cuddling her doll in her arms as if the doll were her baby. Lilli wondered if she would ever have a baby of her own, but she was feeling that she might have Amanda as a child of her own someday soon.

Chapter 60

Grayson and Lilli left very early on Monday morning and traveled to Otwell to make arrangements for the burial of the Hortons. They each had packed a few clothes to wear while they were away from Mabel's house.

Grayson had planned to have a long talk with Lilli about their future, but he quickly realized that this was not the time. He felt that he needed to make sure that Lilli's family was taken care of before he gave her any new information.

As they drove through rural Pike County, Grayson remarked at how pretty the area was. There were vast fields that apparently were planted with wheat and where corn would be planted in the spring. The forests, although barren in the winter, he envisioned being green with summer leaves. He could only imagine how beautiful they would be in the fall of the year. He had never experienced such splendor in nature, having been raised in a city.

Lilli began to talk as they traveled along. She had never allowed herself the luxury of thinking much about her childhood. She had always had a question in her mind about her heritage, but she had hidden it in the back of her mind. Now that she knew the answer to the query, she could relax and think about things that had been hidden for many years.

She shared with Grayson the times when she had

attended Otwell High School. It was a small school with very few students. She and Vickie had been inseparable all during those school years. Because they lived near each other, they could walk back and forth to visit each other. Then the thought came to her; what about Vickie's parents. Did they know the truth about her?

"Grayson, she said, how have Vickie's parents reacted to her illness?"

"I have never told them about what is wrong with her. It would destroy them, I know. I have only said that my schedule would not allow me time to travel and therefore we could not visit. They have not seen Amanda since she was about three years old. I will need to handle that problem in the near future."

"I once knew them quite well, and they are lovely people. I am sure that they would love to have some contact with such a beautiful granddaughter."

Grayson continued to drive on, holding inside the things that he had meant to discuss with Lilli on his visit this time. "I know that I should have made them aware of the problem, but it would have only hurt them. Somehow, I just couldn't do that," he said. "Although Amanda would benefit from their companionship, I couldn't involve her without revealing Vickie's condition. It was just a hard decision to make. I guess I chose the easy way out," he responded.

Chapter 61

The two arrived in Otwell and had to ask directions to the funeral home. Lilli couldn't remember just where it was. The town had changed a lot in the span of time that she had been gone. A kindly man who was seated on the bench in the park told them which street to take to find the mortuary. He looked at Lilli and asked, "Aren't you Miss Lilli, the Horton's daughter?"

"Why yes, I am," she replied.

"I sure am sorry for your loss, he said, they were fine folks. Mr. Horton had not been himself lately. He seemed to be going crazy. I guess he really was. I sure hope Mrs. Horton didn't suffer none. But to die in a fire is really a bad way to go," he continued.

"Yes, I know," Lilli replied, "they were always good parents to me."

As Grayson drove on when, he noticed that the conversation was a bit painful for Lilli to handle.

Chapter 62

Inside the mortuary, the undertaker met them at the door. Lilli looked him in the eye and realized that this man was Kenneth Armstrong, a young man from her high school class. He recognized her and extended his hand to her. "I am so sorry Lilli that our first contact since graduation is in this manner."

"Oh, Kenneth, I am too. This is such a shock. I hope that Mother didn't suffer. Do you know if she did or not?"

"No, Lilli, neither of them would have even known what happened. They would have died of smoke inhalation before the fire would have burned their bedroom. Your father left a note which I saved for you. I doubt that he planned to die in a fire, but he apparently knew that he was sick and probably wouldn't live long."

Lilli took the note in her hand and began to read it.

Dear Lilli:

I am so sorry. My headaches have been so bad lately and sometimes I am not myself. I loved you and your mother very much.

This farm was given to us, now we give it to you. You can do as you wish with it. The brass key to the house is in my dresser drawer. Treasure it because it is the key that your father gave to us, and now I give it to you.

Love always,
Father.

Upon reading Father's last request, Lilli broke into tears. When she saw him last, he was belligerent and hateful to Mother. Maybe we didn't understand the nature of an illness that took away one's reasoning ability. Kenneth handed her a 'fire burned' brass key. "I took the liberty of searching around in the ashes to see if I could find the key. It was in the ashes of the chest of drawers where he kept his clothes."

Kenneth Armstrong took them into the room where they could choose a casket. There were very few remains of the two of them, so they could not hold an open casket for viewing. It was devastating to Lilli, but she now knew the explanation for Father's actions.

Grayson and Lilli selected caskets for the bodies and then left to visit the church in order to make arrangements for the services.

Her friend, the preacher, was at the church and he assured her that they would be buried in the church cemetery. She asked if there was room for them by her birth-mother, Lula Elayne Jackson. The three of them walked to the graveyard and noted that there seemed to be room for two more graves. In fact, the preacher mentioned that there was also one for her birth-father, if he were ever found. Lilli said nothing. She did not want to reveal what she knew about George Jackson at this time.

All the arrangements were made; the burial was to take place on Tuesday, December 27, at the church. Grayson and Lilli thanked the preacher and then they proceeded to go to the farmhouse where she was born. Kenneth had told her that the house had stood empty for several years. Her father never wanted anyone to live in it. He had always told them that rats had probably set up residence there and it might be uninhabitable. She took the brass key and tried to see if it would still open the door. The key worked and Lilli stepped inside the house where she was born but hadn't spent one single night in it. When she looked down the road, the house that once had been her home was now a blackened pile of bricks and charred lumber.

She turned and explained to Grayson that her chores always included gathering the eggs. On some occasions, she had to help milk the three cows that they had when she was young. She glanced into the barnyard and noticed that there were now 5 cows to be milked and it appeared that one of the neighbors was out there right now, milking one of them. She saw a flickering lantern which she knew was an indication that someone was tending the farm animals.

Just as the funeral director had predicted, the house that had been locked for several years, was inhabited by a colony of mice and possibly rats. It was cold and dark inside but Grayson had found some wood out in the back yard and was busily trying to get a fire started in the old cook stove. He checked the well outside the back door and found that there was water in it, so he proceeded to bring some water to heat. Surely there is coffee or tea somewhere in the cabinets, he thought. While Lilli was perusing the rooms, Grayson was planning on how he could make her more comfortable in the old house.

Lilli looked at the bedroom and discovered that someone had left clean linens in a drawer. She picked them up and realized that they smelled a bit musty, but after shaking them a bit, she could see that they could be used on the bed. When she looked at the bed, it appeared to be a bit lumpy, but she was sure it would have to be the best that they could do for this night. She continued to busy herself in checking to see what the old house could offer. She soon discovered that the old outhouse was still standing and she shuddered to think that she had to revert back to that old experience of making her daily trips to the old ram-shackled building.

When Lilli returned to the kitchen, she found that Grayson had managed to prepare some tea for them although there was no other food that the rats had not eaten, so they sat at the old table and prepared to enjoy their afternoon tea. She noticed that Grayson was staring out the window toward the back yard and the farm that extended to the hillside. "What are you thinking about, Grayson?" she asked.

"I was thinking that this farm is definitely the place for a family. Surely someone would want it as a place to raise a family."

"I loved this small town when I was a child, but when I began to grow into a young adult, there were too many unanswered questions. No one would ever tell me the story of why my name was Jackson and my parents' name was Horton. I always felt that I was an illegitimate child of Mother's before she married Father. I was convinced that she was embarrassed by the truth and that explained why she wouldn't ever tell me the story. Now that I know the truth about my heritage, I find this farm a 'homey' place to be."

Grayson took her hand and led her to the big round table that had served as the dining table for her family so long ago. "Please sit down, Lilli, I have some things that I want to share with you."

Lilli pulled up the chair that no doubt her real mother had sat in when she was the 'lady of this house'. She stared into her tea cup and felt that she was slipping into a nostalgic mood. She wondered if the answer to all her questions were lying in the bottom of the tea cup. Grayson sat in the chair that she was sure George Jackson had probably sat In to eat his breakfast each morning. Grayson leaned over to her as he began to talk.

"The reason that I wanted to visit you during the holidays was because I had some things to clarify with you. First, let me begin by saying that Vickie and I were never married. When we left the college shortly after graduation, it was our intent to marry. We came through Otwell and said goodbye to her family as we traveled to Bloomington. We planned to be married on campus before I enrolled in medical school. However, there never seemed to be the right opportunity. As we began life together in the same apartment, I realized that Vickie had never 'given up' Tom Howard. She cried for him every day. She refused to admit that he was the scoundrel that you and I both knew that he was. She saw him as her 'knight in shining armor' and that he would re-surface someday and take her away. She began a regimen of drinking and depression. I tried to help her, but I was very busy studying in Med school and it took most of my time. I realize now that I probably neglected her but we lived together as a brother and sister. We never lived as 'man and wife'. I really tried to help with Amanda to give her a decent life; however, her mother did not seem to care one way or the other for the child. When we moved to Terre Haute, I thought she would 'snap out of her doldrums' but it didn't happen. Then she began to consort with the Chinese, and the rest is history. So you see, Lilli, I am free. I am not a married man. At least, not yet. I want YOU to marry me. I have loved you since our days in college, but I love you even more now. You must understand, I come to you with baggage. I did promise Vickie when she became aware that she was addicted to Opium that I would always care for Amanda. If you will agree to marry me, then Amanda is part of the package. Will you marry me, Lilli, baggage and all?

Please say yes."

Lilli could hardly believe what she was hearing. She began to think that maybe those boxes of unopened mail had explained this story to her and she, foolishly, had chosen not to open them. Now the information came as a shock. "Oh, Grayson, I really didn't know all of this. Of course I will marry you. I have waited so long. You once told me that you would live with Vickie until the child was raised and then you would divorce her and come to me. Do you remember what I told you then?"

"Yes, Lilli, you told me that you didn't want 'used merchandise'. Well, my dearest, you aren't getting 'used merchandise'. I am still the young man that slept with you when we were in college. I have been true to you all these years."

Grayson scooted his chair away from the table and stood beside Lilli's chair. He took her face in his hands and kissed her tenderly on the lips. Then he led her to the bedroom of her real mother and father where the two of them renewed their old romance. Lilli fell asleep in his arms just like she had longed to do for so many years.

Chapter 63

When the early morning sun began to shine through the windows, Lilli heard an old rooster crowing. She knew that it was time to get up. There were always going to be things to do on the farm. Suddenly she realized that Grayson was in the kitchen stirring up the fire. Was he going to make breakfast? She realized that he had been cooking meals for morning breakfast for Amanda. She thought about the fact that she had relied on Mabel to prepare her breakfast. If Grayson didn't fix their meal, then they might have to eat oatmeal. She and Amanda were only skilled at preparing that for breakfast. Before she could decide what was going on, she could smell bacon cooking. She hurriedly found a robe and bedroom slippers from the closet and padded out to the kitchen to find her lover.

"Do you have my coffee ready?" she asked. Then she realized that Grayson had surely been to the store in town to buy supplies for their breakfast.

"Of course I do, and I soon will have a big breakfast ready. I am not very skilled at cooking on this old wood stove, but I am making the best of it."

"When we marry will you promise me that you will put in a bathroom and a modern kitchen in this place?" Instantly, Lilli realized what she had implied with her question. Quickly she turned and hurried out the door to the old 'outhouse'. She would have to think about what she had just said to Grayson. When she returned, he was waiting at the door for her and he wrapped his arms around her before she could say a word.

"Yes, my dear, I will make such a promise to you. You see, you read my mind without realizing it. While you were sleeping last night, I began to put together a plan. I wanted to present it to you this morning, but it seems that you must have had a dream about what was on my mind. I would like for us to move to Otwell and live on this farm. I can set up a medical practice in one of the buildings in the downtown area. I am sure that this town needs a good country doctor. The funeral director assured me that there was a hospital in Jasper where I could treat patients that needed more care. I am sure that the county needs a good qualified teacher. I understand that they are going to build a new elementary school in town in the near future. There would possibly be an opening there for you. And, more importantly, Amanda could get to know her grandparents whom she has not seen since she was a baby."

Lilli sat down in the same chair that she had used the night before. She felt that if she didn't sit down, she would faint. Grayson came to her, as he had done the night before and held her face in his hands, again. He slowly kissed her again, then stepped back and said, "what do you have to say about all this, my dear?"

Lilli never dreamed that she would return to Otwell. She loved living in Evansville, but she quickly realized that she had no other friends there except Mabel. She knew that she didn't have friends in Otwell either, but if she moved back, many of her old acquaintances would surely still live in Otwell.

"What will we do with the farm if I go to work teaching?"

"We will rent the land to the neighbor who has been tending it. He would probably be happy to continue farming it and pay us a portion of the profit. Amanda would love learning how to gather eggs and milk a cow. We can grow a vegetable garden in the summer and plant blooming flowers in the yard. If I promise to have a man install a bathroom and modern kitchen, will you agree to return to your home?"

Lilli stood to her feet and wrapped her arms around this wonderful man. "Oh, yes, she cried, I would love to return to my home. I thought you would never ask," she laughingly replied.

The couple finished their breakfast, cleaned the kitchen, packed up their belongings and left the old, yet newly acquired home of Lilli Jackson.

It was time to go to the church for the funeral for the only parents that she had ever known. The church was sparsely filled with only the closest neighbors. Lilli remembered only a few of them, but they were all very sympathetic with her loss. She heard the preacher tell about what good 'folks' her parents had been to the church and the community. She heard a young woman sing "Amazing Grace" from the very choir loft where she and Vickie had sung as young girls. She wondered who the child might be and decided that she would find out later in order to send a note of thanks to her. When the time came for the family to view the remains, Lilli stood by the side of the casket and cried tears for a family that she had loved so long. She realized that, as in her birth, George had given them all that he had, now in their death, they had given her all that they had. It was a full circle. Her tears burned her cheeks to think that life had been so cruel and yet she was so blessed to have a home for herself, for Grayson, and for Amanda. It was going to be a good day, after all was said and done.

They buried the two nearly empty caskets in the cemetery near the woman who had given her life for Lilli. The well-wishers gathered in the back of the church where they had prepared a feast for the young couple. The conversation among the mourners was of times past, but no mention was made of George Jackson. The questions were there but not spoken audibly. Grayson and Lilli assured them that they would be returning soon to establish a residence in the community. Grayson was sure that the couple was leaving them with material to talk about from now until they returned. As a couple, they expressed their gratitude for the help of the neighbors as they said good bye to Otwell for a few short months.

Chapter 64

On their way back to Evansville, they stopped by the farmer's house that had been tending the farm, inquiring if he would continue taking care of the farm animals until school was out in the summer. They didn't discuss their complete plans with him, but only assured him that he could put out another crop this spring.

When they returned after school was dismissed, they would let him know what the future could hold for him. He readily agreed. Grayson asked if he knew someone who could handle the job of installing a bathroom and a modern kitchen in the old house. The farmer stated that he would love to have the job since farming in the winter didn't pay very well. Grayson and Lilli sat down with him at his kitchen table and drew out the plans for him to follow to add another bedroom, bathroom, and a new kitchen. Lilli also wanted more windows but he was not to remove the front door where only the big brass key would fit the lock. Grayson wrote him a sizeable check to cover the expenses and gave the farmer information on how to find him if he needed more instructions or money.

The two young lovers returned to the car and started down the long road to Evansville. As they traveled along, there were many decisions to be made. They would need to discuss their plans with Mabel. She would be anxious to help them plan a wedding. They would be married by the preacher in Mabel's church out of respect for her. The wedding would be in June at the end of the school year. Amanda would be part of the wedding party. Grayson would need to notify the other doctors in his office that he would be leaving in June. The year was 1930 and the two lovers were 30 years old.

Grayson's car was a comfortable ride as they continued to drive toward Evansville. They found a little café where they stopped for lunch in Oakland City. Lilli discovered that Grayson had an affinity for coconut cream pie. She would have to get Mabel to teach her how to make one. She smiled to herself knowing that it would not be an easy task since she really didn't know how to cook much of anything, especially coconut cream pies.

Chapter 65

When they arrived in Evansville, Mabel had been expecting them. She wanted to know all the things that had happened on their sad trip to Otwell. "Well, Mabel, you won't believe what happened in Otwell," Grayson began. "But, first, where is my baby girl?"

"Oh, she is across the street playing 'dolls' with the little girl who is visiting with her grandmother over there. She will be home a 5:30 p.m. She met her while she was playing outdoors one day. They discovered that they both had received dolls for Christmas so they began to play together. One day they were over here and I had a tea party for them. Today they are over at the other grandmother's house. Yes, and I assured Amanda that I would be her grandmother while she visited here."

"I am glad that we have a few minutes to tell you some of our plans before Amanda returns," Grayson began. He proceeded to explain the details of their plans to Mabel. She was both shocked and surprised at his revelations but she was obviously quite happy. When he came to the part about them returning to Otwell to live, it was obvious that Mabel felt a twinge of sorrow. She had grown so fond of Lilli that she didn't want to see her move away.

About the same time that dinner was set out, the front door burst open and Amanda came running in calling for Lilli. Grayson laughed to see that he was no longer number one in her life, but he had been supplanted by Lilli. Amanda began to babble on and on about the good times that she had been having as she played with the other little girl whom she called Susan.

As soon as the meal was finished, Grayson began to talk to Amanda in terms that he thought she could understand about their future. He explained that he and Lilli were going to be married. Amanda did not mention her mother or the thought that he was already married. Apparently, in her young mind, she didn't care or didn't understand those details. Also, she had not seen her mother in about 3 years, so was mostly unattached to her birth mother. As soon as her father explained that he was marrying Lilli, she leaped into her lap and began to hug her. "Oh, Lilli," she cried, "I have always wanted you for my mother. I know we will have a wonderful life together. I am really tired of my daddy's cooking. I hope you can cook better than he does." Lilli laughed and hugged the child as hard as she dared. "I am afraid, Amanda, that I am not a very good cook, but I will learn if you will help me."

The 'foursome' continued to list their plans for the summer. It wasn't long before Amanda became bored with their adult conversation and kissed them all goodnight. She took her beloved doll and crawled into the bed announcing that she was going to sleep with Lilli again tonight.

The rest of the evening was spent ironing out the

details of what was going to happen between now and June. Grayson was quite agreeable to most of the plans that the women were discussing. He walked over to Mabel and told her that this event was at his expense. He handed her three one-hundred dollar bills and mentioned that if she needed more, she should contact him. Lilli tried to complain and stated that she had money in the bank. "Your money isn't any good right now," he said. "I have made this decision on my own, young lady."

Soon the entire group decided that it had been a long day. Mabel went to her room, and Lilli passionately kissed Grayson goodnight, then joined her 'soon to be' new daughter in the bed.

Chapter 66

School continued after the Christmas break. Grayson and Amanda returned to Terre Haute stating that they would return before June to finalize all their plans. Grayson knew that he was going to have to make some sort of long term arrangements for Vickie, but he wasn't sure what they would be. Should he move her to Jasper where they could look in on her occasionally? That would mean that he would have to reveal to her parents her real condition. Should he just abandon her at the sanitarium since she hardly knew him any more? He couldn't get his hands around that option. He had taken her on as his 'charge' when they had left school and announced that he intended to marry her. He didn't think that he could morally abandon her now.

When he returned to the hospital to work, he discovered that there had been a rash of suicides while he was gone. It seemed that many businesses had begun to fail because of what appeared to be a downturn in the economy. Many men could not see how they could continue to feed their families without an income so they chose to kill themselves. In some cases, there had been a small insurance policy that would pay their widows a sum of money, but quite often, they left their families to fend for themselves. From the case load that the hospital had experienced, they were able to save some of the men. A minister was called in to try to counsel the men on how they could continue to care for their families.

Grayson had stepped in and worked day and night to help the staff with the overload. He had very little time to think about Vickie or Amanda. He was working day and night.

Spring was just around the corner and he wanted to return to Evansville to visit Lilli over the Easter holidays. As a poor substitute, he had called her off and on at Mabel's. Unless the work load would lighten a bit, he was certain that he would not be allowed to take the time off from the hospital to make the trip. He purposely did not mention the trip to Amanda because she would not let him sleep a minute until the day of their departure arrived.

He had visited the sanitarium one morning to check on Vickie. She seemed more lethargic than usual. He knew that the attendants were giving her more and more of the drug in order to keep her sedated. However, she did recognize him and began to cry when he came into the room. He walked over to her bed and asked her if she would like to go to Otwell to visit her mother. She shook her head no and began to cry audibly. "I will take you there if you want to go," he said.

"No, no," she cried. "I never want to see them again. I don't want them to see me like this. Go away, and leave me alone. Don't come back." With those words, she turned her head toward the wall and covered her head with her blanket.

Grayson turned and walked out her door, wondering what he should do now. She had insisted that he leave, but did she realize what she was saying? How could he just leave her like that?

He went back to work at the hospital with a heavy load on his shoulders. Not only did he have Amanda's welfare to consider but he needed to consider what she would say ten years from now knowing that he had left her mother in a sanitarium to die. Would she blame him? He silently wondered how he could have ever gotten himself in this dilemma. He was reminded of a phrase "Oh what a tangled web we weave, when first we practice to deceive." He remembered that the quotation was attributed to Sir Walter Scott. He wondered who Mr. Scott had been deceiving. His deception of Vickie's parents of their sham marriage had been the beginning of his entanglement now. And, yes, he had woven a tangled web.

Grayson was thankful for a busy schedule at work to help him leave his personal life at home until he could arrive at a suitable solution.

Chapter 67

Back in Evansville, the two women were busy night and day with wedding plans. Mabel agreed to make Lilli's wedding dress. The two women haunted the fabric stores for suitable fabric for a wedding dress. Lilli had insisted on a pale rose color for the dress. She did not want to divulge her reasoning behind her decision not to wear white. She thought that Mabel probably realized that she and Grayson had slept together in the past, so she didn't think that she needed to confess their pre-marital behavior. She simply insisted on a pastel color for her dress. Amanda would be the only attendant and her dress would be a light yellow color fashioned similarly like the bride's dress.

Mabel received permission from the pastor at her church to hold the wedding there. Because the wedding was scheduled for June, there would be plenty of spring flowers in bloom that could be used to decorate the sanctuary. Mabel had a few friends who might want to attend. Most of Lilli's students and their parents would be invited, also. Although it was to be a small wedding, there probably would be nearly 100 in attendance. A small reception would be held in the basement of the church immediately following the ceremony. Plans were being made for this event also.

Suddenly, Easter was right around the corner. The winter weather had abated and the spring flowers were blooming everywhere. The dogwood trees were in full bloom and most yards were aglow with tulips blooming. Lilli was sure that Grayson would be back for another visit before the wedding but he had not told her when it would be. In the calls and letters that he had been writing to her, he only talked about how busy they were at the hospital. He hardly made mention of another trip to visit with her.

On Thursday, prior to Easter Sunday, Lilli received a call at the principal's office. She had never received a call there and she had no idea who it could be on the other end of the line. Her stomach hit rock bottom when she thought it might be from Grayson or that something had happened to him. When she answered the phone, it was Grayson on the line. "Lilli, he said, Vickie passed away this morning. She had apparently been hoarding her pills that they gave her at the sanitarium. When she felt that she had enough to make an overdose, she took them all at once. The doctor said that she probably had 10 or 12 in her possession. I am taking her body back to Otwell and will bury her in the church cemetery. Is it OK if I bring Amanda to you for a few days? I can't leave her alone and I don't think this is the time or place for her to go to Otwell." He hesitated and waited for an answer to his request.

"Of course it is fine, I would love to have her for our Easter celebration. Do you want me to accompany you to Otwell?" she asked.

"No, I need to do this alone. I think that I will take the time to explain to her parents the whole story.

Then you and I can begin our lives fresh and without reproach. I believe it will answer a lot of questions about why Amanda has not been to see them, or why Vickie had never returned for a visit. I will see you tomorrow and will bring Amanda for her visit. Just remember that I love you," and with that statement he hung up the phone.

Lilli returned to her class and made an effort to return to teaching them their spelling words. She had just lost her best friend yet Lilli was forced to continue as if nothing happened. She wasn't sure if this made life less complicated or more so. She only knew that she had to finish this day of school and hurry home to discuss all this with Mabel. Grayson would be here on Friday, Good Friday, and she would get to see him again, albeit a promised hard day for him.

Chapter 68

Lilli hurried home to share with Mabel the plans for Easter weekend. Naturally she was excited that Amanda would be there to share their holiday with them. Mabel tried to ease Lilli's concern over not being able to accompany Grayson when he met with Vickie's family. She kept telling her that this was Grayson's problem, not Lilli's, and that he needed to handle it in his own way.

The women continued to work on their plans for the holiday weekend but now it would include a child so some changes needed to be made. Mabel had planned a nice holiday meal after church, but now she felt that she needed to plan to have a small Easter egg hunt for Amanda and Susan in the yard. She also felt that she needed to plan to have an Easter basket filled with candy eggs for the child. Lilli immediately stated that she would handle that task, then she went to her bedroom. She searched through her parcels which she had stored under her bed and found a basket that had been given to her many years ago on an Easter Sunday. "A new ribbon and a few flowers would bring it up to date and be a proper basket for Amanda," she stated. Mabel quickly agreed with her assumption and returned from her sewing room with bits of ribbons and fabrics to update the basket. The women fell into gales of laughter when they realized how seriously they had taken the arrival of a young child for the Easter holiday.

While they were scurrying around trying to prepare for the events, Lilli noticed that the little girl that Amanda called Susan was playing out in the yard across the street from their house. She quickly hurried across the street to inform the grandmother that Amanda would be there for a few days. Susan ran inside and brought her doll out for Lilli to see when she heard that Amanda would be there for a visit. "Will she bring her doll?" the child asked.

"I am sure that she will, Susan, and I know that she will be anxious to play with you again. We are planning on having a little Easter party on Sunday afternoon and we hope that you will join us."

The grandmother looked a bit dismayed. "I have nothing to contribute for a party, she said, since my husband has lost his job."

"You need not contribute anything. This is our party and Susan is invited to play with Amanda."

Lilli hurried back across the street and informed Mabel that she would look under her bed for another basket to give to Susan. Mabel laughed and replied that Lilli might be considered a magician if she could produce another suitable basket.

When the two women completed their tasks of creating Easter baskets from two unused containers from under Lilli's bed, they seemed to fit the needs nicely. The women then went about boiling eggs, coloring them with food dye, and making candy to wrap and include in the baskets. It was nearly midnight when the two of them gladly collapsed in their beds to get some sleep. Lilli wondered how many more happy moments her future might hold as she prepared to become a mother to a young girl. It was a happiness that she never expected to happen this way.

Chapter 69

Grayson arrived in Otwell and went straight to the home of Vickie's parents. He really hated to bring the bad news to her parents, but he was the only one to do it. He had met them only briefly when they had gone through Otwell on their way to Bloomington when he had enrolled in Med school. He had visited them one other time when Amanda was about three years old before Vickie had become so addicted. When he drove up the driveway, her father came out to meet him. He remembered him and quickly invited him into the house. Vickie's mother offered him something to drink. Grayson stated that a good cup of tea would be fine.

He sat down across the room from her parents and stated that he had a long story to tell them. He first stated that Vickie had passed away. The two of them began to weep. He rose from his seat and attempted to console her mother. When they could control their emotions, he began to tell them the long story of what had happened over the past ten years. He hesitated when he got to the part about her drug addiction. He found that extremely hard to explain. Her father quickly picked up on his hesitation. "Was she addicted to some sort of drugs?" he asked.

"Why yes, Grayson answered, but why do you ask?"

"We received a few letters from her over the

past few years. In them, she mentioned that she was having trouble with medications. Did you give her the medications?" her father asked.

"No sir, I did not." Grayson knew then, that he had to tell the whole story. He had not wanted to discuss her pregnancy by Tom Howard, nor their 'pretend marriage' but it seemed that it was going to be imperative that he divulge all the sordid details. "What kind of information did she mention in her letters?" he asked.

"She only said that she had some friends that had given her some medicine and that she seemed to need more and more of it to stay well."

Grayson explained that he felt somewhat guilty because he was so busy in Med school that he may have neglected her. However, he was glad for the opportunity to be able to omit the part about their sham marriage.

"I will make the arrangements for the burial if you want me to. I will pay all the expenses since she was the mother of my child," Grayson stated.

"Where is our granddaughter?" the grandmother asked.

"She is staying in Evansville with an elderly friend of mine that I met in college. She loved Amanda and there is a young girl across the street from my friend that Amanda plays with on many occasions. I will bring her here to visit you very soon."

"I think that Vickie did not want you to see how

serious her addiction was; therefore she chose to stay away from anyone who knew her well", Grayson continued. "As I stated, I was so busy in school and then as a doctor, I am sure that I failed her in many ways. I pledge to you that I will bring Amanda here soon and we will all be together again."

"Did you hear about the Horton family?" Vickie's father asked. "That was such a shame. No one expected that kind of a thing to happen here in Otwell. And did you know that the child that they raised was not really theirs but was given to them upon the death of the mother? That girl was one of Vickie's best friends when they were growing up, but I guess no one ever told her that she had been given away at birth." Grayson could hardly believe what he was hearing from this man. If Vickie's family had known the truth about Lilli's birth, and had never shared it with Vickie, what a travesty that had been. How much simpler Lilli's life would have been if she had known the truth long ago? Vickie's mother went on and on with the sordid details about the death of Lilli's mother and about her father's disappearance. Grayson feigned ignorance of the whole event. He felt that no one who knew him had attended the service at the church for the Horton family. He considered that a blessing in disguise.

Grayson received their permission to plan the funeral for Vickie. He stood up to leave and assured them that he would return soon to let them know when the service would be and where he chose to bury her.

When he got back in his car, he was relieved that his meeting with Vickie's parents went as well as it did. He had really been apprehensive about what he would need to tell them to gain their trust. It appeared that he had won their support and that they were happy with what he had told them about her life and death.

Chapter 70

The funeral for Vickie was held on a Monday morning and she was buried in the same church cemetery where the Horton's were buried. Grayson chose a burial plot on the other side of the church from where the Horton's were buried. This was probably his best course of action without causing any unanswered questions from attendees at the service.

Grayson went back to Vickie's home and assured her parents that he would be back in the summer to bring Amanda in order to get acquainted with her grandparents. He chose not to tell them at this time of any of his future plans about returning to Otwell to live or his relationship with Vickie's best friend, Lilli.

He got in his car and began his long trip back to Evansville. He made a quick stop at the house that was being remodeled for the 'newlyweds'. He found the carpenter in the house, and saw that the bathroom was nearly completed. The carpenter had already installed the kitchen and a sink. There was a faucet lying on the countertop. Grayson wondered how the faucet would fit into the plan. The carpenter explained that he was going to put an electric pump on the well and the kitchen sink would have running water inside. Grayson explained to him that he wanted another room and bath installed on the back of the house. He gave the man more money and made no more explanation. The carpenter expressed his surprise that the house would have two bathrooms, but Grayson insisted that he follow his instructions.

Grayson returned to the car and continued down the road to Evansville to see Amanda and Lilli. He would have very little time to spend there because he needed to get back to work at the hospital. He also had to settle Vickie's debts with the sanitarium where she had spent the last 3 years of her life as a helpless invalid. He had many things on his mind as the fields of green wheat growing flew past his car windows. He realized that Lilli's farm fields were probably green too, and he was sorry that he had not checked on the farm while he was in Otwell. He simply had other things on his mind at the time.

Grayson turned on the radio to listen to the news as he traveled on toward Evansville. The news commentator was giving the news of the day. It wasn't very good. The news man was saying that many companies were closing their door and that thousands of men were out of work. He thought about his own life as a doctor. He would always be needed. Lilli was a teacher and she would always have a job. What he didn't realize was that many people would not be able to pay a doctor for his services or that many counties would not have the funds to pay teachers for teaching their classes.

He traveled on. It was dark before he reached Mabel's house. Only then did he realize that he had missed the Easter celebration. Amanda met him at the door with many stories to tell him about her experiences finding Easter eggs and the tea party that she had enjoyed with Susan. Mabel and Lilli had hosted the party for the two girls. She produced the Easter basket that she had received on her pillow Sunday morning; all of which Grayson was happy to hear about. He wanted to discuss with the women what he had heard in Otwell but Amanda was too wound up to go to bed at this time. Mabel offered a treat of cookies and milk in an effort to calm the child. Instead of tea, the 'foursome' gathered around the table for cookies and milk so that Amanda could go to bed.

"Before you head to your room, Amanda, I have something to discuss with you," Grayson began. "I buried your mother today. She had been very sick for a long time. Amanda hardly knew how to respond to the news about her mother. "But, Daddy, I don't remember her much," the child answered.

Oh, I have some other news for you. Lilli and I are going to be married. She will be your new mother." Before Grayson could say anything else, Amanda had jumped into Lilli's lap and was hugging her with all her might. "I'll love for you to be my mother. I haven't had one for a long time. My mother was very sick."

"Amanda, there is more to the story. Lilli and I are going to move to Otwell to live. You will be able to visit your other grandparents. Lilli also has a small farm in Otwell. There are chickens and cows on the farm. You can learn to feed the chickens and milk the cows. Does that sound like fun?"

"Oh, Daddy, I think that having chickens and cows sound like more fun than I can imagine. When will we be moving?"

"As soon as school is out and we have the wedding. We will move to Otwell and begin a new life."

Grayson turned to Mabel and stated that she had just heard their plans. He assured her that they would expect her to come and visit when she could but he made no other statement concerning the house in Otwell. That would be his secret. With that statement he took Amanda by the hand and tucked her in bed, kissing her goodnight. She was quite excited about the prospect of having a different life, although she knew that she and Grayson would leave early in the morning to return to the hospital to work. Like Amanda, he really had no idea about living in the small town of Otwell or any other small town.

As soon as the child was in the room attempting to sleep with her Easter basket and her doll, Lilli returned to the parlor to hear about his trip to Otwell and his visit with Vickie's parents.

Grayson gathered his thoughts together and began to tell all about the details. He left out the part about them having knowledge of Lilli's parentage. He thought that he would divulge that at a later time. He mentioned that he had buried Vickie on the other side of the church, since it appeared that there were no more spaces on the same side where the Hortons' were buried.

He discussed with the two women the news that he heard on the radio about the number of men out of work. Mabel concurred and said that she had read about some of the factory closings in the morning paper. No one seemed to be concerned that this news might affect them.

Chapter 71

The school year ended for Lilli and she said goodbye to all of the other teachers and the principal at the school. She was excited about beginning a new life with Grayson.

Mabel and Lilli had worked their 'fingers to the bone' preparing her dress and the dress that Amanda would wear for the wedding as well as another one for Mabel. There were lots of preparations made for the small reception that was to be held In the church basement after the ceremony. Most of the other teachers from her school planned to attend the wedding and the reception. The secretary had agreed to assist at the reception by cutting the cake and pouring the punch.

Amanda and Grayson planned to arrive on Friday evening. The wedding itself was scheduled for Saturday afternoon. Everything at Mabel's house was on schedule and the anticipation of the events was almost electrifying. If all went well, the wedding will be over, and then the new family would move to Otwell. Grayson had managed to keep his secret from Lilli about the extra room added to the house. He had been in contact with the carpenter from time to time. And he assured Grayson that all the work would be completed by the date of the wedding. He also assured him that he had plowed the fields and started a garden near the old burned out house. "The garden plot there is more fertile," he told Grayson. "that plot will grow lots of potatoes and beans if they were planted at the right time," he continued.

Chapter 72

For Lilli, it seemed like a million light years before Grayson and Amanda would arrive. She was so anxious to see them and to begin their life anew as man and wife. She knew that all the preparations were complete and that there would not be any complications on the big day. She could hardly imagine what was ahead for her. She had never been a 'mother' to anything. Soon she would be the surrogate mother of a child who could not remember even having a mother's influence.

She would need to teach her to sew her own clothes and to tend to chores on the farm; but most of all she would need to teach her how to be a woman. She needed to make Amanda understand that she was loved by her new 'mother'. Just thinking about life with a young girl made her happy to have this new opportunity. She had been teaching young children for several years, now she could teach her own child.

Lilli made one last trip through the kitchen to make sure that the cake and punch were completed as planned. She scanned the table to make sure that the silver ladle was polished to perfection. Then she returned to her room to make sure that her clothes were properly packed and ready to make the trip to Otwell as soon as the reception was over. She had cleaned out her room of all the things that she had accumulated while she lived there and made it ready for the next person to occupy as she had done for so long. Mabel had been such a good friend to her and she knew that she would miss her very much. She could hardly imagine how she could function without Mabel as her confidante. She knew that Grayson would soon fill that place in her life, but she was convinced that she had room in her heart for both of them. She really hated to say goodbye to Mabel.

Chapter 73

Grayson and Lilli were married on the first weekend of June, 1930. Grayson. Amanda stood proudly by Lilli as her assistant, soon to be mother. The minister proudly pronounced them man and wife, stating that Grayson could now kiss his bride.

The reception was beautiful with all the spring flowers surrounding the table and cake. The visitors mingled throughout the room and talked to everyone in attendance. Grayson's parents came from Mt. Vernon to see their son marry his long term sweetheart. Their gift to the new couple was financial and a promise that they would visit soon in Otwell.

When the crowd had cleared the church, Lilli, Amanda, Mabel, and Grayson hurried to clean up the spoils of the celebration. Grayson had announced that they would not be leaving for Otwell until morning. He did not want to travel during the dark of the night.

Lilli prepared their celebratory tea for everyone, and they all gathered around the Mabel's dining room table. Amanda hurried across the street to tell her friend, Susan, goodbye and that she would be leaving early in the next morning. While she was gone, Grayson made his announcement to the two women.

I have taken the initiative to add a room to the house in Otwell. We want you to join us there, Mabel. We need you to help with Amanda and to be another grandmother to her. Lilli will return to teaching as soon as she can get a job in the area, and you can help us run our household. "Please tell me that you will say yes." With his words, he reached across the table and took Mabel's hands in his.

Lilli had had no advanced information about his having chosen to build an extra room, but she began to weep when she realized that the woman who had become her closest friend over the past few years might be accompanying them to Otwell.

"What will I do with my house in Evansville?"

"Surely it will sell to some young family," Lilli said.

Take a month or so to make the arrangements for your move to Otwell. We will come back and get you at that time. Let's plan on the 4th of July for your moving date, but if you need a few more days, we will wait."

Grayson, I have not had a real family since I lost my husband and son. I enjoyed having all my young tenants in the room that I chose to rent after my husband died. None of them were as close to me as Lilli has been. I shared all her stories that she chose to discuss with me and I also learned to love you and Amanda. Without talking about it any more, my answer is 'yes', and I will be ready by the Fourth.

Chapter 74

Morning came early because the newly weds wanted to travel to their new home and their new life together. Lilli could hardly wait to see what Grayson had commissioned to be done while she had been finishing the school year.

She packed her belongings in the back of Grayson's car and put her clothes in her own car. She would follow him as they traveled up the road.

She went back into her room and took a pen from her purse, found a note pad and wrote none last letter.

George Jackson

c/o C.& E. I. Railroad

Vincennes, Indiana

Dear George:

This letter will notify you that Mr. & Mrs. Horton were burned to death in a fire at their home a few months ago.

I have married my long time friend from my college days. We are moving to Otwell and will live in the home where you and my mother once lived. The 'brass key' still works on the front door.

I hope that you and Barbara will come to visit us. I'm sure you remember where the house is.

Your daughter,

Lilli Jackson Parton

Lilli sealed the letter, placed a stamp on the envelope and asked Mabel to post it for her when the mailman came by the house.

She pulled the door to her room shut behind her and walked out to her car, started the engine and headed east to Otwell to return to the place where it all began.

THE END

OTHER BOOKS

The Jewel of LaFlore County

Emily's Quest

The Roosevelt Family of Southern Illinois

The Making of Mary Ann

A Tangled Web

The Secret of the Old Red Bridge

The Secret of the Old Stone Chapel

The Secret of the Old Grey Barn

All About Harry

Yesterdays Remembered - Vol II

CPSIA information can be obtained at www.ICGtesting.com
Printed in the USA
LVOW05s0816010714

392478LV00002B/7/P